Angel *Without* Wings

MARI MANNING

author of *Holding Out for a Hero*

CRIMSON
ROMANCE
F+W Media, Inc.

Published by
Crimson Romance
an imprint of F+W Media, Inc.
10151 Carver Road, Suite 200
Blue Ash, Ohio 45242

www.crimsonromance.com

Dedication

Prologue

Pick me! Pick me! Pick me! The three letters on Linnea Basinger Reyes's desk pleaded for help.

She hated this part of being Senator Kenneth Klein's "angel" so much it made her stomach ache. All three deserved a check from the Helping Hand for Colorado Veterans fund, and if she had her way, they'd get one. But Ken put his foot down. Pick one big story with enough buzz to revive his re-election campaign.

Blotting out the ringing phones, the urgent voices, the campaign office hustle-bustle, Linnea ran her finger along the ragged edge of the letter ripped from a spiral notebook. It wasn't fair that two orphaned sons of a fallen officer couldn't afford college. She slid her eyes to the neatly typed letter beside it. How could she bear to turn away a young father who lost his wife in a helicopter crash and needed to move closer to his parents?

She lifted the third letter. The mauve paper reminded her of a bruise. The waves of black ink rolled across the page like a stormy sea. The story sliced through her like a razor. The name at the bottom made her stomach twist with shame. Adam McCormick.

A movement caught her eye. Ken was back from lunch. She shuddered. He stood amidst the jumble of desks, nodding seriously as one of the campaign assistants read him an item from the *Post*. He waved at Linnea, and she pushed a smile to her lips so he didn't see her revulsion.

Her gaze dropped to the purple stationery. It was all wrong for Ken's campaign. A complicated problem—no children or puppies—but she was choosing it anyway. *Cheater.* Without lifting her head, she watched Ken turn away and disappear into his office. She started to breathe again, and blood rushed back to her brain. Marco had left her a little inheritance. She'd send it to the other families.

Linnea studied the portrait of her husband on the cabinet beside her desk. Marco's dark eyes stared back at her, as enigmatic and unyielding as ever. His expression somber, befitting his uniform. The picture dwarfed the one in the dented frame beside it. Marco's arm was slung across the shoulder of Adam McCormick. They wore Ray-Ban sunglasses and desert fatigues and grinned into the relentless Afghanistan sun unaware that before the week ended, one of them would die and the other changed forever.

She yearned to tear the photo to pieces and get on with her life. But first she had to make amends for what she'd done to Adam McCormick.

Chapter One

Linnea let go of the steering wheel and stuck her hand into her purse. An envelope's sharp corner poked her palm.

"Ouch!" A warning to turn around and go home? She wanted to.

Sign the divorce papers, Linnea ...

No, Marco, please give me another chance...

Let me go, puta, it's over...

I can't.

Infuriated, Marco had hung up the phone and led Adam into the ambush that cost Marco his life and Adam his future as a complete man.

Digging the purple envelope out of her bag, she double-checked the address: 110 Canyon Road, Cloud River, Colorado.

Canyon Road turned out to be a sad, crumbling ribbon stretching across the east Colorado plain. Grayish ranch homes on wide lots of brown grass and dingy snow lined the faded pavement. How had Adam felt when he finally came home? Relieved? Depressed? Empty, the way she did?

Topping a low rise, a burst of turquoise drew her eyes, and the brightest house she'd ever seen shimmered in the morning light. Three greenhouses trailed behind it like glass boxcars. Puffs of smoke curled from the brick chimney. It sat in a pretty little valley, cozy and tucked safely away from an unpredictable world just as she always imagined a home should be. No wonder Adam's family was fighting to keep it.

She parked Marco's old Silverado in the gravel driveway behind a dented green delivery van with Cloud River Organics—Food for Life stenciled on the side. Linnea frowned at her worn jeans and sheepskin boots, not really appropriate for an official campaign visit, but she came as soon as the check was cut and before Ken asked where she was going.

A quick moment to size up the house—sprawling, one-story, wide windows, cheerful, friendly—then she grabbed her shoulder bag and jumped out of the truck. A set of shaky porch steps moaned as she skipped up the planks, and the absence of a doorbell required a sharp rap on the heavy oak door. She pressed her ear against the cold wood. Nothing stirred on the other side.

No footsteps except hers marred the fresh snow. Someone must be home. Tramping across the lawn, she leaned over a wide juniper bush, squinting against her own reflection to peer through the wide window.

"Who are you?"

Linnea jerked up, and her feet slipped on the icy grass. For a few seconds she was airborne before crashing to earth with a teeth-shattering jolt. When she raised her head off the ground, a tall, dark-haired man was frowning at her from the open door.

He stepped off the porch and ambled over. The unlaced work boots that stopped inches from her side were big and worn. Her eyes traveled over a pair of long legs encased in faded jeans and slid across the stretched fabric of his blue tee shirt to his broad-shoulders. He was gorgeous. Warmth spread across her cheeks at the thought.

She peered up at his face. Dark brows, arched in surprise, topped green-gold eyes. Tiger eyes, hunter eyes, unwavering, intelligent, hungry. A spasm of longing skittered through her, and she sidled her gaze away from his to study the black beard stubble framing a generous mouth, which at this moment was agape with surprise.

He had to be Adam's hell-bent older brother.

"I'm guessing you're not a cat burglar," he said.

"Sorry. I didn't think anyone heard me knock."

"Wasn't expecting anyone." He offered her a work-roughened palm. "Can I help you up?"

Wet snow seeped through the back of her jeans, and her ankle throbbed. "Thanks."

He grabbed her hand, his palm warm against her wet, icy fingers. She barely had time to register the frisson of pleasure when he hauled her to her feet. A sharp pain shot up her leg, and she nearly toppled sideways.

"Whoa, whoa, there." His arm slipped around her waist, and he pulled her against him. "Are you all right?"

"I don't know. My ankle hurts." She leaned heavily on his shoulder as she balanced on her good leg, and he barely stirred. Solid as a tree, but much more enjoyable to rest against.

He scowled at the wobbly ankle. "Try standing on it."

She straightened her knee and gingerly touched the ground with her toe. Then she shifted her weight. It hurt like hell but held. "I must have twisted it a little."

"Can you drive?"

"I think so."

"Good. I'll help you to your truck. When you get back to the bank, put ice on it. Then tell them we'll have the mortgage money in a few days."

"The bank?"

"You're not from the bank?"

"No. I'm here to help you."

His scowl deepened. "You're going to help me?"

"I got Adam's letter."

"Adam wrote you a letter asking for help?"

"You didn't know?"

He shook his head.

"He said his brother—I assume that's you—was being forced to take a dangerous job as a mercenary—"

"Adam!" His voice shattered the air and shook the snow from a nearby pine.

"What, Jesse?"

She swiveled her head toward the familiar voice, and her throat constricted as Adam McCormick emerged from the house. He was so thin, and his brown eyes—his warm, lively brown eyes—were sunken and ringed with fatigue. His body hung heavily on a set of metal crutches. Her gaze dropped away from his face. The left leg of his jeans was empty below the knee. Her eyes slid away, and her cheeks burned with shame. She'd known he'd be different, but the reality was worse than her nightmares.

"Do you know this woman?"

"Hi, Linnea." The ghost of a smile played on Adam's lips.

"Hi."

"She says you contacted her." Jesse met her eyes. "What did he want again?"

Her uninjured ankle wobbled from doing the work of two, and Jesse's heavy arm squeezed her waist tighter every time he asked a question.

"I'm sure this can all be cleared up if Adam and I can talk privately," she said.

"Not on your life." Then Jesse propelled her into the house. "We'll talk inside."

An exotic hodgepodge of handicrafts and art crammed the wide front room of the McCormick house. Macramé webs dangled from the cathedral ceiling. Rustic oak shelves filled with primitive clay vessels and figurines teetered along the sides of the room, and blood red Navaho rugs covered the worn pine floor. A dozen life-size bronze sculptures of children at play were scattered around a tiny island of furniture adrift in the exotic sea. The aroma of cinnamon curled through the air.

Linnea inhaled deeply. If she ever had a real home, it would be cozy and colorful just like this one. "It's so bohemian."

"Yeah, that's the McCormicks for you." Jesse didn't sound pleased. "Come join us in the Kasbah."

Using Jesse's body as a crutch, she limped to a sofa covered by a bright gold afghan while trying to ignore his solid male body. Two worn easy chairs, a coffee table strewn with books and a big screen TV completed the circle of furniture. "Have a seat." Jesse slid his arm from her waist, and she dropped onto a worn cushion.

Adam swung into the house and poked the door shut with the tip of his crutch. Jesse narrowed his eyes at his brother. "Do you want to tell me what is going on?"

From the back of the house, a disembodied female called out, "Why are you growling, Jesse?"

A moment later, a woman emerged. Tall and willowy, she seemed to glide into the room. Thick black hair threaded with silver rippled down her back, and a jade green caftan embroidered with spring flowers floated around her. But the bright blossoms didn't camouflage the dark circles beneath her luminous brown eyes. She had to be Corrine—Adam and Jesse's mother. Corrine reminded Linnea of Murphy, her own mother. She'd had been beautiful, too, but Linnea had watched her fade into a papery shadow, so thin when she died that Linnea could scoop her up and carry her.

"Didn't mean to disturb your meditation," said Jesse. "We'll try to keep it down. Got a little excited is all."

Corrine's gaze fell on Linnea. "We have a guest. Why didn't you tell me?"

Jesse sighed. Adam swung through the room and dropped into an easy chair. Corrine floated past the bronze statues, patting their heads like the Old Woman in the Shoe soothing her children. She sank down on the sofa beside Linnea.

"Are you a friend of my sons'?"

Linnea glanced up at Jesse. He'd propped one broad shoulder against a small patch of open wall. From beneath knitted brows he glowered at her. The gold sparks glittered when she met his eyes. A man who took care of himself and those in his care. It was stupid for her to come.

"Adam and my husband served together in Afghanistan."

Jesse and Corrine turned to Adam. He smiled at Linnea again. His brown eyes were warm. "That makes us friends. Thanks for coming."

Jesse shifted his weight. "You aren't here to visit Adam."

"I got the letter Adam sent to the Fund. Your story touched my heart." She pulled the letter from her shoulder bag.

Jesse reached across the coffee table and snatched the letter out of her hand. She tried to grab it back, but he stepped out of her reach. "Let's enjoy the tragic tale of the McCormicks together," he said.

Adam took a sharp breath.

Corrine pressed a hand to her chest. "That's private, Jesse."

Jesse unfolded the letter. "How private can it be since everyone seems to know what's in it but me?" His eyes skimmed down the page, darting from one line to the next, his expression growing thunderous.

"Dear Linnea." Jesse's gaze flicked across her face. "Last year Robbie—my father—died, and we had to take out a mortgage on our organics farm to pay his medical bills. Our farm fell on hard times since we were fixated—" He lifted his eyes from the page and stared at Corrine.

She stopped fidgeting, folded her arms across her chest and lifted her chin defiantly.

He continued. "—fixated on Robbie. We are about to lose our house and our farm. We are not whining. We'll eat cat food if we have to—" He stopped. "I'll skip the rest of this drivel. Let's jump right to the good stuff, shall we?"

Adam looked away. Corrine bent her head.

"A few weeks ago my brother informed us he was joining a paramilitary security company to earn the money to get us on our feet again. They will send him to Colombia. He's replacing a guy who died so this is a dangerous assignment, plus he would be gone for two years. We are both veterans so when my mother and I read in the newspaper about Senator Klein's fund to help veterans and how you were in charge we decided to write you. Please buy our family a little more time to get the farm going again. We know things will get better, and—"

Jesse broke off and glared at Adam and Corrine. "You two should be court-martialed. Begging strangers for money. Turning private family matters into fodder for politicians. Where is your pride? And you—" His eyes narrowed into Linnea's. Her heart did a little flip. "—should get in your truck and go back to Denver or wherever you came from. This family pays its own way. We don't accept charity."

He balled up the letter and flung it over her head. It hit the window, landing on the floor with a soft crunch. Snatching a canvas coat off the curls of a bronze boy carrying a pail of berries, he strode to the door.

"Where are you going?" Corrine sounded on the verge of tears.

He didn't turn around. "Outside. To watch our farm fall on hard times!" He banged the door shut behind him. The sound bounced off the flock of bronze children and echoed through the room like tiny bells.

Chapter Two

Jesse smashed through the greenhouse door and tried not to mind the loud creaks as it gave way, then snapped closed behind him.

"Mornin', Jess." Kevin Burke, the farm manager, sat on a camp stool playing a game on his phone.

"Aren't you supposed to be loading the van?"

"Just taking a little break." Kevin's black eyes glittered with resentment as he stood and stomped down the herb aisle to the flats of hydroponic lettuce waiting at the far end.

Damn! What was wrong with him? He seemed to be snarling at everyone these days. But nothing had turned out the way he planned.

When he was kid, he'd dreamed of flying. The best day of his life was getting accepted at West Point. He'd horrified his hippie parents, but he'd loved the army and flying choppers, even when he was dodging missiles in Afghanistan. Stateside he had a great apartment near the ocean and a beautiful lady. Capital L on lady.

Then his life turned into a house of cards. Robbie got sick and couldn't manage the farm so he lost his contract with the local organics distributor. The old supermarket in town was their last client. Last spring Adam was wounded during his first tour. Robbie died a few months after Adam was brought back to the States. So Jesse requested a hardship separation from the army. Now he was jobless, apartment-less, lady-less, and one day from signing away two years of his godforsaken life to get Corrine back on her feet.

This morning, the cherry on top of this mess landed on his front doorstep. She reminded him of Alice in Wonderland, except she was definitely not a little girl. Pale blond hair that brushed her waist, gray eyes big enough to drown in, a sweet, slender body that curved under his palm. Jesse's jaw tightened. She was as naïve and meddlesome as the real Alice. A paltry donation was not enough to fix their problems. They needed a lottery's worth of money.

"Hey, Jess."

Ashley Cooper pushed through the doors. Jesse gritted his teeth. Not this again.

"I'm so glad I found you." Her blue eyes blinked at him from a frame of thick mascara as she swayed into the greenhouse in a ridiculous pair of spiky boots. Her curvy hips, sheathed in something tight, blue, and shiny, knocked a wide trestle table holding dozens of Corrine's delicate peppermint and lavender tea seedlings. The tiny pots rocked precariously, and two lavender plants landed on their side. Queen Ashley didn't notice.

"Ash, I'd like to visit, but I'm slammed." He bent and righted the pots.

"Of course. This will only take a teeny, tiny second."

He sighed and turned away from her. "Walk with me, then. I've got to help Kevin load the lettuce."

The hollow clack of her boot heels on the concrete floor quickened behind him as she scurried to catch up. When she reached him, the scent of her flowery perfume hit his nostrils. He sneezed.

"Bless you." She managed to give her benediction and sound annoyed at the same time. "I hope you're not coming down with something."

"Typhoid."

"You're such a tease, Jess. Seriously, we have to talk."

He pulled up short. "Look, Ash, it's not my—"

Her smile faded and her eyes glittered like marbles. "No, Jesse. *You* look. No one around here wants to pay up the wazoo for organic crap. I'm willing to give Corrine a very generous offer for this useless piece of land. She can pay off the bank and whatever else she owes. Plus we'll knock down the greenhouses and that turquoise eyesore for free and cart away all the stupid junk inside. It's not like buyers are lining up for this place."

"It's not my call. We've been through this already."

Ashley held up her index finger and wagged a red nail at him. "May first, Jess. Then our offer drops. Five thousand each week. We're trying to be fair. Generous, really. If the bank forecloses, we'll get this place for nothing at auction. Corrine has to understand."

"She'd be selling out to the Man. That's what she understands."

Ashley's eyes narrowed.

"I'll be gone by the middle of April. She can't run the farm by herself. I predict she'll sign on the dotted line before I land in Colombia." He mentally crossed his fingers. Nothing would make him happier than to dump the old place and collect a six-figure check from Ashley freaking Cooper. With the money he'd make flying choppers for Keystone Security, he'd pay off the mortgage and the tax man, plus put aside enough money to assure Corrine a life of modest comfort.

"Will Adam try to stop her?"

"He's doing eight to midnights at the radio station and driving up to Fort Collins three days a week to school. Besides, he's in no condition to run this place." Jesse attempted a lopsided grin. "Can you do me a favor, Ash? Be patient. She's going to come around."

"She better. I'd hate to see your mom lose out on the money. I love this little valley. You know that, Jess. But Daddy wants me to scout out other locations for the new development so Corrine better not wait too long to make up her mind."

"She won't. I have to run."

Ashley batted her spidery lashes at him. "I'm staying in tonight if you want to stop by. We can watch a movie or something."

Or *something*. "I'll try."

*

The crunch of Jesse's boots on the gravel drive faded away, and silence fell over the room. Round-eyed, Adam and Corrine gaped at the front door. Linnea dropped her head and studied her feet.

Adam broke the silence. "What do we do now?"

Now? Linnea jerked her head up. "Your brother made his feelings clear. He doesn't want my help."

"Jesse is still driving up to Winter Park tomorrow to sign the contract with Keystone Security unless we stop him."

"Come on, Adam. He's not going to change his mind. You heard what he said. No charity."

She turned to Corrine for confirmation, but Corrine swung her head away and looked at Adam. Something unspoken passed between mother and son.

Adam cleared his throat. "I could sure go for a cup of your mint tea, Corrine."

Corrine sprang off the sofa. "How rude of me! I'll put the kettle on." She scurried away.

Slouched in a patched brown lounger beside the sofa, Adam's mouth curved into an easy smile when Linnea looked at him. Did Jesse's mouth curve the same way when he smiled? If he smiled.

"I can't force him to take the money. I'm sorry, Adam. Honest."

"I know."

He grabbed his crutches and pushed himself up, then pivoted on his foot and plopped down next to her. The cushion wobbled like a choppy sea. "I'm glad you came. I guess you must miss Marco a lot."

"I guess."

Adam tilted his head and considered her. Whatever he read in her face made him nod. "I know. It's not even a year." He dropped his eyes to his lap. "I knew you'd help us out when you read our letter. I remember how nice you were when I dropped in for dinner last year. Marco told me once you had a soft heart."

Marco hadn't meant it kindly. Her need to help others made him impatient. *Why do you let people take advantage of you?*

This trip had been a bad idea. How did she expect to make up for a lost leg? An interrupted life? She should hand him the check and go before she made a mess of things for his family. Forget the article for the *Denver Post*. Forget the campaign publicity. She'd figure out a Plan B later. If Jesse wanted to risk his life in Colombia, it was none of her business.

Adam drew her back to the present. "I hate asking for charity just as much as Jesse." He smiled his sweet smile.

Her resolve disappeared. "Please don't think of it as charity, Adam. Think of it as payback. You and Jesse have sacrificed so much, it's the least we can do." *Jeez.*

"It's okay to call it charity." His voice softened. "I'm doing this for my mother. Corrine has been through so much this past year, and all she wants is for our family to stay together in our own house. I'd jump in and help Jess with the farm, but, well—" He trailed off.

If it wasn't for her stubbornness, he could. "I should go before Jesse comes back." She held the check out to him. "Please take the money. Whatever your brother decides, this will help you and Corrine a little."

When Adam didn't move to take it, she dropped the check in his lap. It fluttered against his knee and fell to the floor, landing under the empty leg of his jeans. She rose and tried to tear her eyes away as she zipped her hoodie. She couldn't. Panic rose from her skin like steam, but she had to ask the question haunting her nearly every night.

"Did Marco suffer?" She barely breathed as she waited.

Adam shook his head. "I don't know. It was over so fast."

"Can you tell me …" The words stuck in her throat. "…what, uh, happened?"

"It was weird day, that's all."

"Weird how?"

"Marco was the best scout we had. The guys called him *El Aguila*."

"The Eagle?"

"Yeah. He knew how to spot artillery from miles away. Guns, too, and bad stuff along roadsides. But he missed the most obvious gun placement ever. He just walked into the ambush, and *El Aguila* Junior, that was me, I followed him."

Because of her. Because she'd refused to give Marco a divorce, and he'd gone out on patrol blinded by anger.

Adam stared down at the check. "We have to stop Jesse from going to Winter Park tomorrow."

"This is between you and your family."

"Please, Linnea." His dark head hung over his mangled leg as he waited. "We need your help to save Jesse."

She owed him a leg … and a real life. Her knees buckled, and she sank down on the sofa. The loose spring groaned. "Jesse's made up his mind. What else can I do?" As she contemplated another confrontation with Adam's brother, her mouth dried.

Corrine appeared, carrying a tray with three mugs of tea and an earthenware plate piled high with plump cinnamon buns. Steam from the mugs curled behind her as she moved, and the grassy scent of mint filled the room. Linnea inhaled deeply, but she couldn't relax.

Corrine set the tray on the coffee table and handed mugs to Linnea and Adam. She carried hers to an easy chair and settled in. "I knew the universe was smiling on us today. I felt the positive forces when I meditated this morning."

"As I told Adam, this is really between you and your sons. I shouldn't butt in. The check will tide you over while you work things out."

"Please help us." Corrine's soft voice touched Linnea. "Jesse's a good man and a wonderful son. But he sees everything as a problem to be solved. He can't understand he's more important to me than money or even the farm."

How did she get into this? "I'm sure you and Adam can talk him into taking the money." She sent up a small desperate prayer.

"But if we can't, he'll go away and maybe get killed, and we'll still lose the farm because there's no one to do the work," said Adam, the man she owed a limb to.

"How can you stop him? We can't very well tie him up. He's strong enough to take all three of us on at once and not break a sweat." The image of a pair of long, powerful legs rose in her head. "If he wants to go to Winter Park, he's damn well going."

One of Adam's brows arched. "Why can't we tie him up? It's only for a day. The guy he's supposed to meet in Winter Park leaves tomorrow night. If he doesn't sign Jess tomorrow, he'll find another pilot for the tour."

"Come on, Adam, it's impossible, not to mention illegal to hold Jesse against his will. Maybe he won't have you arrested, but what about me?"

"Once the recruiter leaves, Jesse will come around," said Corrine. "He's been doing a lot of barking lately, but that's not really him. He's just worried."

Adam leaned forward. "Corrine and I have a plan, but we'd nearly given up on pulling it off. It requires a stranger to, ah, do the heavy lifting."

"This morning I asked the universe to send an angel to save Jesse," said Corrine. "And here you are."

If she'd really been an angel, Linnea would have restored Adam's leg, then spread her wings and fled Cloud River like a bat out of hell. But she wasn't.

Chapter Three

"It's right over there." Corrine pointed to a squat yellow-brick building floating in a sea of faded blacktop. As the Silverado sailed past the supermarket, Linnea glanced in the rearview mirror. An illuminated plastic sign announcing Cloud River Food Mart perched on the roof. The green delivery van wasn't among the sparse collection of cars in the parking lot.

"Looks like Jesse's not there."

"He's unloading lettuce today. The van's parked in back," said Adam.

"Of course." Her heart sank. "I'll turn around at the corner." Slowing the Silverado, she hung a right on First Street. Her eyes nearly popped out of her head at the quaint downtown. "This is unbelievable!"

"Welcome to Cloud River," said Corrine.

Linnea slowed the truck to study the little shops in colorful Victorian houses and ornate brass street lamps hugging the brick sidewalks. On one side the Mother Earth Café took up three storefronts. Beside it stood a flower shop with a giant wooden tulip hanging over it. Next to the flower shop was a bakery whimsically named The Muffin Man. The Potter's Wheel displayed rows of earthy green pitchers and vases, while tall apothecary jars filled with herbs and spices heralded The Colorado Spice Company. Further down, a white clapboard church rested on a patch of grass dotted with weathered gravestones. Across the street, an old stable held the Cloud River Brewery. A flock of BMWs, Infinitis, and Escalades were parked in front.

"The brewery seems to be popular," she said.

Corrine's voice was tight. "City people. They live in the Cooper's McMansions. Cloud River's their dude ranch. They get to feel like cowboys and fishermen and such only with four-car garages and chain stores."

"They're trying to rezone the church property so they can bring in a big supermarket and discount store," added Adam. "If that happens, all these shopkeepers will be out of business."

Linnea made a U-turn and headed back. At the edge of the old downtown, a Georgian building with Doric columns rose like a dignified sentry. A discreet brass sign over the door read "First Bank of Cloud River." The silence in the truck grew thick.

"Let's get back to the supermarket, shall we?" Linnea punched the gas pedal and steered the Silverado back onto the highway.

At the supermarket, she squeezed the truck into a narrow space close to the entrance. Her ankle was still sore, plus Adam couldn't manage a long hike with the prosthesis he'd strapped on, and Corrine, who'd changed into a pair of jeans that hung in folds on her thin frame, was so fragile, a strong gust of wind might blow her away.

Linnea put the Silverado in park and faced Adam and Corrine, who were wedged into the front seat beside her. "We're here so you can convince him to accept the money and stay in Cloud River. Agreed?"

Corrine nodded solemnly, but Adam narrowed his eyes. "You're not getting cold feet, are you?"

"Your plan is illegal."

"So is speeding, but I noticed you were going seventy on the highway."

"Come on, Adam. It's not the same thing. If Jesse presses charges, I could end up in jail." If Jesse pressed charges, the story would land on the front page of the *Denver Post*. Ken might lose his re-election bid.

Adam's eyes softened. "We agreed to reason with him first. It's only a last resort, or, what did you call it?"

She raised her eyes heavenward. "Plan B."

Corrine patted her arm. "Plan B. I like the sound of that. It's hopeful." Her expression sobered. "Don't worry, Linnea, Jesse is too kind-hearted to press charges. He'll forgive you."

Highly doubtful, but arguing was getting her nowhere. She pulled the keys from the ignition. "Come on. Let's get this over with."

Paint peeled from the supermarket's window frame, and the yellow brick was nicked and scraped from the rusted shopping carts. The automatic doors squeaked as they swung open. Inside, the walls were grimy, the lighting fixtures old and dim, the linoleum floor yellowed with age. In the produce area, duct tape held together a chipped enamel scale beside display bins scratched to a misty white.

Amid this decrepitude, Jesse and a heavy-set guy set out little bunches of bright green lettuce. They both straightened up when she walked in beside Corrine and Adam. Jesse seemed even taller and broader than she remembered. As she approached him, something hard settled in his eyes. Beads of sweat rolled between her breasts and over her stomach. *This man could be dangerous if crossed.*

Jesse's companion brushed dirt from his hands. "Hey, Adam. Corrine."

Corrine and Adam shot him half-smiles. "Hey, Kevin."

Jesse's eyes swept the circle of faces. "Mind setting out the rest of this batch while I grab another flat from the van, Kevin?"

"Sure."

Jesse jerked around. "The rest of you follow me." Corrine and Adam shuffled after him, and Linnea reluctantly followed. Jesse stopped before a metal door with "Employees Only" painted across it. His eyes locked into Adam's. "What are you doing here?"

Adam's confidence seemed to slip. "We ... we came to talk to you."

Another bead of sweat rolled down Linnea's belly. *Take the check, Jesse. If you don't, then it will be worse than you can imagine.*

"About?" asked Jesse.

"Look, Jess, we know you're worried. We all are. But Linnea has agreed to help—"

"Great." Jesse held out his hand to her. "Let's see it."

She blinked. "The check? Really?" Relief poured through her.

"Isn't that what you came here to deliver?"

Anger rolled off him in waves. If this was his idea of surrender, Plan B—if she was forced to go through with it—was guaranteed to erupt into more fireworks than the average war zone.

"Are you sure you understand what you're agreeing to?"

Jesse's gaze narrowed. "I'm not agreeing to anything. I want to see the check."

Adam stepped forward. "We can do this, Jess. We just need a solid plan to make the farm profitable."

A tiny muscle at the corner of Jesse's mouth twitched. But his hand stayed palm up. Waiting.

She sighed dramatically and gave in. Her fingers shook as they slid into her shoulder bag. "Have it your way. But if you take the check, you must stay in Cloud River. That's the deal." She should mention the feature article she was supposed to write for the *Post* on the chosen veteran. That was part of the deal, too. She met Jesse's eyes. They were darkened by impatience. First things first. She pulled out the check and waved it at him. "Here."

The rectangle of pale blue paper, loosely clasped between her thumb and forefinger, hung between them. Jesse glared down at it. Then he took it and tore it in half.

"What are you doing?" She snatched the precious pieces from his hands. "That's a cashier's check!"

He tilted his head and read the amount. "It's not enough."

"Jesse, please." Corrine pressed a thin hand to his shoulder. "It's enough to get us through the spring at least."

"You haven't paid property taxes since Robbie died, and we haven't sold enough produce to pay the mortgage since when? Halloween?"

Corrine nodded.

"That's more than four months. How long do you think the bank will allow you stay at the farm for free?"

Corrine looked up at her son, wide-eyed. "I don't know."

"Look around you. This place is on its last leg. Even if I could sell enough organics here to pay the bills, how much longer before they knock down the old church and build a new supermarket? And you know it's going to happen. Money trumps everything else. What are you going to do when that happens?"

Linnea's scalp began to tingle. Plan B was closing in on her.

Adam tried again. "That's why we need the money. So we have time to figure out our next step."

Jesse drew back his shoulders until the hard plane of muscle under his tee shirt bulged. "Decision time ended a long time ago. Tomorrow I'm driving up to Winter Park to sign the papers, and when I come home, I will have enough money to pay off the mortgage and taxes on the farm with something left over to keep Corrine going until she agrees to sell to the Coopers. Now go home!"

"No!" It was Corrine. Anguish etched her pale face. "I can't lose you. Not after your father and the worry when Adam was wounded. I can't face any more."

"What about the farm? How can you just give up like this? It was Robbie's dream," asked Adam.

Jesse's face softened. "I'm sorry." He pulled Corrine against him and laid a hand on Adam's shoulder. "Wouldn't he sell the farm if it meant your security?"

They didn't answer.

Jesse sighed. "You're going to have to sell the farm before it loses any more money, Corrine. It's as simple as that."

"No!"

"You can rent a place in town and—" The clash of metal on metal rocketed through the store followed by the clatter of dozens of toppling cans. "For chrissake, what now?" asked Jesse, but his feet were already moving.

Linnea hurried after him, but as she quickened her steps, Adam whispered, "Plan B."

*

An ear-splitting scream nearly blew out Jesse's eardrums as he knelt on the crusty supermarket floor picking up cans of green beans and corn. He jerked up his head and twisted around. That friend of Adam's— the girl who looked like Alice in Wonderland—was screaming louder and longer than he'd ever heard any woman scream in his life.

Nearby, Corrine comforted the weepy mother of the boy who used a grocery cart as a battering ram. As Alice's screams morphed into high-pitched screeches, Corrine slid an arm around the mother's shoulder, took the kid's hand, and ushered them both to the end of the aisle where Adam was calmly watching Alice—why couldn't he remember her name?—scream her head off.

A dozen curious shoppers pushed close to Alice and Jesse, as well as Kevin who was helping with can retrieval. One of the townsmen, Harry Burgetti, stepped forward. What was he doing here in the middle of the day? His daughter Hannah couldn't run The Muffin Man by herself. "Aren't you going to help this girl, Jesse?" He twisted the tip of his thick mustache.

"I guess." He jumped to his feet and stepped close to Alice. The scent of herbal shampoo filled his head. He backed up half a pace. "What's wrong?"

"You stole my wallet!" Wide gray eyes that reminded him of rain clouds met his gaze. His breath hitched. Then she took a deep breath and let rip another ear-splitting scream.

He struggled for equilibrium. "That's ridiculous."

Her mouth snapped open. "Help me! Someone please help me."

An ominous buzz rose from the crowd. His body thrummed with adrenaline. "Stop screaming." He pressed his hands against her shoulders. The bones, light and fragile beneath his palms, yielded. Her big eyes rounded with fear.

She wrenched herself from his grasp and faced the other shoppers. "I had three hundred dollars. Someone call 911."

A girl in a tight Cooper Construction tee shirt waved a pink cell phone in the air. "Already called."

This was a nightmare. He tried to get in front of Alice again. "Look at me. What are you trying to do?" But he already knew. Corrine and Adam were going to get him locked up until Keystone left Colorado, and they'd conned this girl into helping them.

Harry pushed him back from her. "It's going to be okay, Jess. The cops are on their way. We'll get this straightened out lickety-split."

Jesse's eyes slid over the other faces in the crowd. All familiar. Mostly friends and neighbors. But a few pairs of eyes studied him suspiciously. Cloud River was a small town. His family's financial woes were general knowledge in these parts.

He peered over the heads of the gawkers. The end of the aisle was empty. Adam had disappeared. Corrine was missing, too. He had to find them. Force them to stop this ridiculous charade. Stepping over cans of green beans, he tried to push through the knot of people. His boot hit one of the cans. It skittered away.

One of Alice's slender fingers pointed at him. "He's trying to escape!"

A strong hand gripped his arm. He jerked around and met Kevin's eyes. A gleam of triumph sparkled in their depths. "Slow down, Jess. I'm sure there's a reasonable explanation for the missing wallet."

Jesse spun on Alice. She pressed her back into the soft sacks of brown rice on the shelf behind her. A knot in her throat bobbed as she swallowed. His eyes narrowed. A thin film of sweat covered her face. Her eyes, round and wary, met his, then slid away. She began to chew on her lower lip. His adversary was nervous. Time to mount a counter attack.

He gripped her forearms and pulled her against him. Her soft body hit his full on, hip to hip, waist to waist, breasts to chest, and it took him a moment to absorb the quiver of excitement and get back to saving his ass.

"What the hell are you doing to me?" Her face was inches from his, and her sweet scent filled his nostrils. She tried to jerk away from him, but he held her tight. His future as a free man was in the balance. "Tell me."

For a split second her body relaxed in his arms. She lifted her mouth to his ear. Her damp breath, smelling of cinnamon and Corrine's mint tea, brushed his ear lobe. "We're saving you."

A roar of anger filled his head, then two sets of hands grabbed his shoulders and pulled him away from her.

"Hey, Jess, what's going on?" Teddy Scripps, his buddy since grade school and now the sergeant of the Cloud River police force, frowned at him. Teddy brushed a hand through his mop of red hair, then he nodded at the deputy who still gripped Jesse's arm. "Let him go."

The hand on Jesse's arm relaxed.

"What's going on?" Teddy repeated his question as he looked from Jesse to Alice and back to Jesse.

"Ask *her*."

"This man stole my wallet, Officer."

"Come on, Teddy. She's lying."

Teddy's eyes narrowed into her face. Her chin rose. "I can prove it."

Teddy turned to the crowd. "Go back to your shopping. Everything's under control. Go back to your shopping, please." The crowd reluctantly dispersed, grumbling as they sidled away.

Teddy paused for a moment as his scanner squawked. Then he faced Alice. "Can I have your name, ma'am?"

"Why do you need my name?"

"If you want to file a complaint, I need your name."

She chewed on her lower lip again before mumbling, "Linnea Reyes."

Ah, yes. That was her name. Not Alice.

"Do you have a driver's license or other form of I.D.?"

"It's in my wallet, Officer." She sounded belligerent.

Teddy's brow creased with displeasure. "This is a serious charge. Do you have proof Jesse stole your wallet?"

"This morning when I went to visit Adam at his house, Jesse snatched the wallet out of my bag and stuck it in his jacket. Then he ran out the door before I could stop him."

"That's bullshit!" The protest roared out of him. "Where's Adam? Where's Corrine? They're my witnesses." When they saw his predicament, they'd give up this outrageous plan ... wouldn't they?

"Calm down, Jess. We'll find them." Teddy nodded at the deputy. "Take a look around. See if you can locate Corrine and Adam McCormick. Find Jesse's jacket." His eyes met Jesse's. "Where did you say you put your jacket?"

"I didn't. But it was on our lettuce flats in produce."

The deputy nodded and hurried off. A few minutes later he returned, carrying Jesse's jacket across his arm. Corrine and Adam followed a dozen paces behind, heads hung low, eyes cast downward.

Teddy took the jacket from the deputy. "Okay if I take a look through the pockets, Jess? Easiest way to clear this up."

A prick of nervousness stung the base of Jesse's neck. "Sure."

Teddy's beefy, freckled hand patted the pockets. "There seems to be something in the right pocket. Did you put your wallet in your jacket?"

Jesse's wallet was in his jeans. "No." Corrine began to fidget nervously, and Adam took a sharp breath as Teddy reached into the jacket and pulled out a pale blue wallet. Jesse stared down at the pretty girl whose name he'd forgotten again. She looked away. He pushed toward Adam and Corrine until the deputy's hand grabbed his arm. Outrage welled up in him.

"Come on, Adam! Corrine! Are you really going to let them take me to jail?"

Stony faced, with deep pain glimmering in their eyes, they silently watched him struggle. Then Corrine reached out blindly to clutch Adam's hand, and it hit him like a fucking speeding train—they'd won. He was going to sit in the Cloud River jail until Glenn Keystone was safely out of Colorado.

He broke the deputy's grip, spun on Alice, and pulled her hard against him. Her face was so close he could have touched her pale cheek with his nose. Her mouth popped open, but he pinned her against the rice sacks with his chest so she couldn't pull enough air into her lungs to scream. Her gray eyes filled with terror.

"This isn't over, baby. You'll pay for this."

Two set of hands closed around his shoulders and pulled him away. But as he was handcuffed and dragged out of the supermarket, he savored the small triumph of seeing Alice sink to her knees beside a sea of dented cans and sob.

Chapter Four

Through the windshield of the Silverado, the lights of Cloud River burned in the valley below. Linnea fixed her eyes on them and tried to forget that the police station was just a few yards behind her. Its dark hulk was an unwelcome reminder of the terrible thing she'd done today.

The look in Jesse's eyes when he understood what she was doing to him. She'd expected anger, but there'd been something else, too. Another emotion had flashed across his face. One she couldn't name. She shook her head slowly, trying to shake the word loose. But it wouldn't come.

The refrain from Supertramp's *Take the Long Way Home* blared as her cell phone came to life. She twisted her head and peered at the caller ID. Her spirits sank further. Senator Klein.

"Hi, Ken."

"Where are you? No one's seen you since you left the campaign office last night."

Her mouth tightened. He didn't own her. "I'm with our veteran family."

"Dammit, Linnea. We were supposed to meet the family together. What the hell are you doing?"

A smile curled her lips. Defiance felt good, especially with sixty-five miles separating them. "I delivered the check today. Their letter sounded so urgent, I decided to go up and scout out the situation. Turns out they needed the money right away so I took the initiative and handled it myself." There was dead silence at the other end of the line. "We'll get a photo of you with the family later."

"Are you sure that's the only reason you went without me?"

31

I went without you because you're a creep. But she didn't say that. "Of course it is. Why else?"

Ken changed gears. "Tell me what happened. How did it go?"

"The meeting with the family went as expected." *Hah!*

"Were they surprised?"

"Uh, very."

"Where are you exactly? Are you coming back to Denver tonight? We can grab a cup of coffee tomorrow, and you can fill me in on the details before I leave for Grand Junction. I'll be out that way for the rest of the week."

Linnea raised her face toward the night sky and gave thanks. That would give her a little more time to clean up the mess she'd made in Cloud River and return before Ken started wondering what she was up to. "I'm spending the night here."

"Why? Is something wrong? Where are you anyway? I'll have my car pick you up."

"No! I mean I don't want to disturb your campaign work. I, uh, I witnessed a robbery at the, uh, supermarket. The police asked me to stick around until it's straightened out."

"A robbery? Are you sure you don't need me?" She could almost hear Ken's frown. He'd be in his mahogany-paneled office, leaning back in his top-grain leather chair, feet up, perfectly polished wing-tip shoes perched on his antique desk. By this time in the evening his silver hair would be a little mussed and his silk tie loosened just an inch or so, which was Ken's idea of relaxing.

"Absolutely not. I'm perfectly capable of taking care of myself." *Like hell.*

Fine-boned knuckles tapped lightly on the truck window. Linnea jumped.

"Linnea? What is it?" asked Ken.

She squinted through the glass. Corrine waved at her. "I have to go."

"Tell me where you are."

"I'm, uh, in a little place near, uh, Greeley."

"Is this that family with mortgage—"

Corrine rapped on the window again. "Gotta go. Talk to you later." She cut Ken off and rolled down the window.

"Is Jesse okay?" Linnea asked. Adam had taken the McCormicks' Honda Civic to the radio station, and the van was still at the supermarket so she'd reluctantly offered to drive Corrine to the police station. A bit too close to Jesse for her comfort, but how could she refuse Corrine?

"He's as good as can be expected."

She breathed a sigh of relief.

A worried frown creased Corrine's face. "He wants to see you."

Linnea stopped breathing. "Me? What for?"

"He said he wants to discuss the terms of his surrender. What should we do?"

"He has to stay put until tomorrow night after eight. We should go."

Tears welled up in Corrine's eyes. "I know I have to be strong, but it's so hard to see my son locked up in jail, even for one night."

Linnea reached through the open window and squeezed Corrine's fingers. They were cold and stiff. "I'm sorry."

Corrine sniffed.

Digging her free hand into her bag, Linnea pulled out a pack of tissues and handed one to Corrine. "Here. Take this."

Corrine dab at her nose.

"I'll bring you back to visit him tomorrow morning. Jump in the cab and warm up. I'll go in and tell Teddy we're leaving."

Teddy stood at the front desk, a pair of reading glasses perched on his nose as he wrote on a clipboard.

"Just wanted to say good-by. I'm taking Corrine home."

He scowled. "I asked you not to leave Cloud River until we get this situation straightened out."

"I'll be around until tomorrow evening." Corrine would need moral support to get through the day. Adam, too.

He set the clipboard down and came around the counter. "Maybe I can get you on your way tonight. Follow me."

"I'd rather deal with this tomorrow, after a good night's rest."

"Follow me."

What else could she do?

He pulled a ring of keys from his belt and unlocked a thick steel door. It swung shut behind them like a clap of thunder. She followed Teddy down a damp, cinderblock hall. The faint scent of urine clung to the gray bricks, and she tried to breathe through her mouth so she wouldn't gag. Halfway down the corridor, light spilled through a two-way mirror set in the wall.

On the other side of the mirror, Jesse prowled a small interview room, his body moving with the tension and strength of a caged tiger. His long legs took the length of the room in four steps before he spun on his heels and headed back in the other direction. The stark room held a rough pine table and two metal chairs. A plastic container of Corrine's stew and a thermos of tea sat unopened on the table.

Teddy spoke from behind her. "I can't bring myself to lock him in a cell. I grew up with Jess, and I've never known him to steal even a paper clip. Shit, he's a decorated army officer. Gave Uncle Sam twelve years of his life if you count West Point. I'm hoping you made a mistake. Maybe in the heat of the moment you mis-saw something, and now you want to withdraw your charges."

She did. But not until tomorrow night. "I … I'm not sure. Can I sleep on it?"

"Jess wants to talk to you. Maybe he can help you see things clearly tonight."

Linnea spun around. Suspicious blue eyes studied her. "Maybe tomorrow would be better."

One rust-colored brow arched. "Jess seems like a man with something to say now."

The fluorescent light from the interview room cast a bright

square on the wall behind Teddy. Her eyes followed the tall shadow moving from one side of the square to the other like an actor on a stage. She felt Teddy's hand press against her shoulder and push her toward the door. Then he opened it and not-so-gently shoved her inside.

"See if you can't work something out tonight." Then the door closed behind her with a loud click.

Jesse stopped pacing. He rubbed his hand against the dark stubble on his chin. His eyes swept down her body, then up to her face. "Alice."

She inched backward until she hit the door. "It's Linnea."

"Sorry." He gestured at the table. "Have a seat." His new steely calm felt more dangerous than his earlier rage.

She crept over to the table and perched on a chair. The metal was cold against her thighs. The back bit into her spine. Jesse slid into the other chair and shoved the container of congealed stew aside with an impatient sweep of his arm. Then he leaned forward.

"Why'd you do it?"

"I don't know."

"You can do better than that. Hell, make something up. You seem to be an expert at tall tales."

"It's complicated."

"I got nothin' but time, lady."

When she remained mute, he pushed out of his chair. Leaning over the table, he studied the top of her head.

"You can make this right, Lin. Just one word. That's all it would take."

She forced herself stand up and meet his gaze straight on. It was part of her penance for Adam's leg. "I can't until tomorrow. You know that."

He shook his head. "This is unbelievable. How old are you?"

It was none of his business, but it seemed sensible to grant a small concession. "I'll be twenty-seven in July."

"Then you should know better. I could haul your ass into court for setting me up, but I'm willing to forget this happened." His voice softened to a gentle rasp. "I know it's hard to resist a poor widow and her wounded son—the two of them get to me sometimes, too—and Teddy will look the other way …"

His eyes turned the color of warm toffee. His words flowed over her like melted butter. "It won't matter whether you withdraw the charges today or tomorrow. I'll still sign on with Keystone and fly choppers to pay off my mother's debts. The only difference is that by the time Keystone is back in the country, Corrine will owe even more than she does now."

"A lot can happen between now and Keystone's return."

"What if nothing happens?"

She bent her head and studied the table. A past occupant had carved a heart into the rough wood with the tip of a blue pen. She traced it with her finger. "Families should stay together." *And she owed Adam this favor.*

"Why?"

The truth about Marco bubbled up inside her. *I owe your brother. It's my fault he's wounded. Everything is my fault.* She swallowed it. "It's how things are meant to be."

"Come on, Lin. Be serious."

"I am being serious." She traced the heart again.

His work-roughened hands curled into fists. "Is that your final decision?"

"Yes."

"Look at me."

She couldn't lift her head.

He slid a finger under her chin and tipped it up. "That's better." The earlier warmth had vanished. He spoke with deadly calm. "When I get out of here, and I guarantee you it won't take long, you better be far away. In fact, you might want to relocate to another continent because there aren't going to be enough places for you to hide on this one."

She couldn't move.

"Get out of here." He growled the words through his teeth. "Go back and comfort my mother and brother while you are still in one piece."

Oddly, the word for what she'd seen in his face at the supermarket came to her. Hopelessness. The recognition hurt more than his outrage and the hot hatred in his eyes that seemed to rain down on her like sparks from a fire. She spun toward the door and pounded frantically until Teddy came.

Chapter Five

"Bye, Adam. I'll call you as soon as I've talked to Teddy."

"Thanks again. Have a safe trip." Adam closed the door behind Linnea.

She stepped outside and zipped her hoodie against the chilly March night. The sky was the color of royal blue velvet, and a full moon cast pale shadows against the McCormicks' gravel driveway. A beautiful night, but it was almost eight. Time to set Jesse free and get the hell out of Cloud River.

"Leaving us already?" A man emerged from the deep shadows behind the Silverado.

Her eyes widened. "Jesse?" She grabbed for the truck door and wrenched it open. As she dived into the driver's seat her arms flailed for the car door, but her fingers clutched the sleeve of a canvas jacket instead.

Righting herself in her seat, she eyed the dark figure looming in the open door warily. "What are you … I mean how did you … You're not supposed to be out."

Jesse lifted a booted foot onto the running board and leaned into the cab. Deep shadows darkened the skin beneath his eyes. Strain creased the corners of his mouth. "Got bailed out early."

Stay calm. Take it slow. "Look, Jesse, I'm sorry this whole thing got out of hand."

Jesse nodded. Draping his arm on the open door, he turned his head away from her and stared up at the moon. "Things got out of hand. Is that what you call sticking your wallet in my pocket, then accusing me of theft in front of the whole town?"

"You know why. You're safe, and your family is together."

"Bullshit."

"Look, if there is any way I can make this up to you …" She shrugged since there was little she could do except call Teddy and drop the charges.

"Now that you mention it, maybe there is. Seems like my manager—you remember Kevin—refuses to work for a common criminal. At least he was man enough to come down to the jail and tell me to my face." Sarcasm edged Jesse's voice.

"You're not a criminal."

He went on as if he hadn't heard her. "So now it's just me, doing the work that used to require four people, five if you count Corrine."

"I *am* sorry. Honest."

"Right this minute I should be relaxing in front of the TV, mortgage paid off, and the organic biz a memory. But because of you, I am broke and back to busting my hump so I can keep up with Corrine's most urgent bills. And do you know what would really help me out?"

She swallowed. "A check from the Helping Hand fund?"

He graced her with a humorless smile. "An assistant I don't have to pay a freaking dime to because she owes me."

"That's insane."

"What you did was insane. What I'm doing is business."

"Come on, Jesse. I can't stay here and work for you. I have a job."

He shifted forward and met her eyes. "That's right, you do. You work for Senator Klein."

This was heading in a dangerous direction.

"What would he do if I contacted him and explained what happened?" Jesse asked.

Ken would fire her, of course. If it ended there, she would be kicked out of the campaign staff apartments and condemned to sleep in her truck until she found another job. She was okay with that. She'd survive just like she always did. But Ken wouldn't end it there. He'd use her disgrace to press himself on her again.

She studied Jesse. He was furious with her. It rippled just below the surface of his skin. So why did she feel safer with him than she did with Ken?

She'd been so stupid, so naïve, to let Ken buy her an expensive gown and escort her to his biggest fundraiser of the year. *Just business. I need a date, and you happen to be free.* That's what he said. Afterward, in the back seat of his limo, he leaned into her. Her evening dress tangled in her legs when she tried to scoot away. The memory of the sudden, sharp pain when he pressed his hand against her breast and squeezed hard hadn't faded with the angry purple bruise. Nor had the sudden crack of his palm against her jaw when he slapped her.

He'd murmured, "We'll have to work on obedience, won't we," as she twisted out of his grip. He must have seen the shock in her eyes, but he smiled anyway. "We belong together. You'll see." He'd hurt her, and that's what he said. She'd been too numb to respond. Linnea watched as Jesse buttoned his coat against the sharp north wind. "How long?"

He dropped his foot from the running board. "Move over."

"What?"

"Move over. It's cold out here."

"Get in the other side."

He laughed. "So you can take off the minute I let go of the door?"

Not with the Ken threat hanging over her head. "I won't. I promise."

"Move over." His tone brooked no disobedience. She slid to the passenger side. Jesse dropped into the driver's seat and shut the door. "Let's see, where were we?"

"How long would I have to stay before you'd feel paid back?" She could probably hold off Ken for a week. She'd text him tonight. Tell him she was still dealing with the robbery situation.

Jesse turned to her. The planes of his face reflected the golden moonlight as he draped an arm across the seat. He smelled of fresh air and pine, and the heat of his arm warmed the back of her neck. "I don't know. What's the going rate for a man's reputation?"

"I know I can never pay you back for what I did, but I can spare a week. Will that help?"

"Maybe." He twisted forward in his seat and reached for the ignition. When his fingers didn't connect with keys, he held out his hand. "Keys."

"Where are you taking me?"

"To the police station. Then right back here. You can stay with us while you work off your debt. Corrine has a big bed, and she gets lonely at night. You can work for me during the day and keep her company in the evenings."

The Silverado roared to life. Jesse shifted into reverse, but he didn't release the brake. His green-gold gaze raked across her face. "Is there someone you need to call? Is someone waiting for you in Denver?"

"No."

"What about your husband?"

She averted her eyes. "Didn't Adam tell you? He was killed in Zhari. It was the same day Adam was wounded. "

He studied her. She sat very still, praying the ugly things in her life stayed securely inside her head where he couldn't see them.

Finally he sighed, and she started to breathe again.

"Okay, then. Good," he said and backed the Silverado out of the drive.

Chapter Six

Beads of sweat ran along the creases curving down the ridge of her cheekbones. Mitchell Basinger glanced at the monitor. Ten more minutes. God, how she hated treadmills. Outside her penthouse windows, a low gray sky hung over Chicago and blocks of ice bob on the waves of Lake Michigan. Ah, for summer and a game of tennis at the Club. But she had no time for tennis since the Old Man died. Nowadays reading dull reports and listening to gray-haired men quote her father to her—without the snarl, of course—consumed her precious time.

After the Old Man's funeral she'd prayed until the skin on her knees was raw that her sister would see the Old Man's obit and know it was safe to come home. But when weeks turned into months and months into years, she stopped praying. Murphy wasn't ever coming home.

She glanced down at the monitor again. Seven minutes to go. She eased the speed down to zero and turned off the treadmill. What was the point? The cancer was back.

*

Mr. Petros stood before a wall of windows, gazing down at the barren tree tops of Lincoln Park. Mitchell studied his back. He wasn't what she'd expected, but then again, Julian had found him. He seemed the sort Julian would know.

She adjusted the skirt of her pearl gray Chanel suit—she was losing weight again—and cleared her throat. He spun around, and she examined his face across her wide room filled with sleek Italian leather furniture that the Old Man would have hated. Mr. Petros's small, sharp features and beady eyes reminded her of a possum.

"Mr. Pos—I mean Petros, please sit down." She swept her hand at her treasured Luna Rossa sofa.

He nodded and approached leisurely, his white running shoes, jeans, and grimy ski jacket out of place against the gleaming parquet floor and soaring windows. He sat, and she joined him. "What can I do for you, Ms. Basinger?"

"Call me Mitty."

He nodded. "Peter."

Peter Petros. Okay then. "I must find my sister."

"Must?"

How to put this diplomatically? If she died before she found Murphy and her children, the Old Man won. He'd always preferred cousin Julian. Two fat peas in one nasty pod.

"Basinger Industries must be headed by a family member. Julian might have mentioned this to you."

"No." His quick little eyes darted around the room, assessing her things.

"The Basinger bylaws are clear about this. Unfortunately about the time the Old—uh, my father—died, Julian ran into some problems so I was elected chairman." More to the point, Julian ran a subsidiary into the ground, and the board had to answer to Basinger's shareholders so they couldn't elect Julian. But they'd wanted to.

He eyed her. "So?"

"If I had to resign, not that I'm planning to, I would like my sister and her children to have a shot at heading Basinger." Let Julian chew on that little tidbit for awhile.

"Tell me about your sister." Peter stuck a hand in his jacket pocket and withdrew a battered spiral notebook. He patted his other pocket then peered at her. "Do you have a pen? I forgot mine."

"Of course." She tried to hide her annoyance as she rose from the sofa, but the sharp click of her heels against the parquet gave her away.

When she returned and handed him her gold Cross pen, he didn't look up at her. She took her seat again. He cleared his throat. "When did you last see your sister?"

"It's been almost twenty-seven years."

He nodded and wrote that in his book. "Where did you last see her?"

"Here." Mitty dropped her eyes to the manicured fingers folded in her lap. "Not here, exactly." This condo hadn't existed then. "At our family home up in Lake Forest." She stretched her neck and watched him scrawl "Lake Forest" on the second line of the page. His hand hovered above the paper, prepared to transcribe more.

She cleared her throat and focused back on her hands. "My sister got pregnant. It was our senior year in college, and when my father found out, he arranged for her to go elsewhere to have the baby. My sister sent me a postcard from Union Station saying not to worry, she'd be fine. I never heard from her again." Only half the story was true, but it didn't matter. Murphy had disappeared. That's the only truth that mattered.

She shifted forward and picked up the manila folder lying on the ebony coffee table. Should she offer him a soft drink or at least a glass of water? No. He might linger, and she wanted to be alone. "There's an old photo in here."

He took the folder from her and opened it. A small black-and-white picture slid out. He caught it before it hit the floor and brought it up close to his face. "Which is which?"

In the photo, two blond girls with eager blue eyes and ponytails giggled at each other. She remembered the day it was taken because of the serious gray-eyed boy behind the camera and how it was the day all of Murphy's troubles began.

"Does it matter? We're identical. Besides, it was taken almost thirty years ago."

He pointed to the girl on the left. "This one has a scar on her chin." He glanced over at Mitty's chin. Hope sprang up inside her.

"That's Murphy. We were playing doubles, and we both dove for the ball. She got the ball, and I got her chin. My sister ended up with nine stitches."

He snapped his notebook shut. "Any idea where she might go? Did she have a friend that moved away? Maybe a place she always wanted to visit."

Mitty shook her head slowly. "No." She stopped. "Murphy would go west if she had a choice. She always said she wanted to live in the mountains." She shrugged. "But maybe not."

He nodded but didn't open his notebook. "Can I reach you here?"

"I'm moving back to Lake Forest for a few months." Closer to the hospital. "My cell and the address are in the folder."

He nodded again. "Good." He stood up and slid the notebook and gold pen into his pocket. She didn't say anything. "I'll keep you posted on my progress."

Chapter Seven

"Is everything okay?"

Linnea looked up from the tiny shoots of lemon balm and lavender she was transplanting for Corrine's tea garden and eyed Jesse. His damp hair was combed, his face freshly shaved. He'd changed into a clean shirt, not one of the tee shirts he wore during the day but a pressed cotton shirt in pale blue broadcloth. She breathed deeply and inhaled the familiar, musky scent of his aftershave—a scent she'd begun to associate with irritation.

"Going out again?"

A dark brow popped up. "Thought I might go into town for a beer."

"You could stay home now and then." It was day four of her servitude, and Jesse had "gone out for a beer" every night.

He glanced over her head at the trays of herbs. "If you fill all the pots with dirt first, it goes much faster. Like a factory line."

She eyed the little clay pots lined up like an invading army extending deep into the shadowy recess of the greenhouse. Either way, she was going to be here until midnight.

"You know what would really make this go faster?"

"I'm almost afraid to ask."

"Some help."

"Tell you what. On my way out, I'll ask Corrine to brew a pot of her ginseng tea. Just the thing to boost your energy."

She pursed her lips and narrowed her eyes.

Jesse took a step backward. "Gotta go. See you tomorrow."

She watched him stride to the door, loose-limbed and lithe, exuding male confidence. Her pulse quickened.

He placed his hand on the door knob, then stopped and turned back to her. "Are *you* doing okay?"

An unbidden smile curled her lips. "A few sore muscles, but otherwise I'm fine."

The truth was she'd never been sorer, more exhausted … or happier. Once she dropped the charges, Jesse's anger faded and the McCormick family absorbed her into their daily routine as if she'd always been a part of them. She drank in their family life and love for each other like a hungry baby with a warm bottle. If only she could freeze her life right this minute, she'd never want another thing in this world.

Jesse let go of the door and came back to her. "I can't figure you out. You have a great job in Denver, you're young…" He paused, and his lips puckered as if he were sucking a lemon, "and you're reasonably attractive—"

"Thanks," she said dryly.

He shuffled his feet uncomfortably. "You know what I mean."

Not really. "So what's your question?"

He studied her until she squirmed. Dropping her gaze, she eyed the oversized army drab tee shirt she wore over dirt-stained jeans. Her hands, roughened by soil and water, hung at her sides. Not a very attractive picture. She sensed his withdrawal.

"It's nothing. I better go." He spun on his heels, and this time he left her alone.

Watching him stride across the yard, she found herself wondering if Jesse ever did anything impulsive.

As Linnea returned to the seedlings, the van's engine roared to life in the front of the house. A few minutes later the Honda put-putted away to the radio station. The kitchen light flicked on, and Corrine's head appeared in the window over the sink. Humming under her breath, Linnea picked up a hand trowel and began filling a row of clay pots with the secret McCormick recipe of soil and compost. As she finished the first row of pots and leaned over the table to work on the next, an invisible finger slid across the back of her neck, and the skin under her ponytail prickled.

Her hand froze in midair over a half-filled pot. The trowel slipped from her fingers, chipping the edge of a clay pot as it clanged against the table. She twisted around.

"Is anyone there? Corrine? Is that you?" Her words echoed through the cavernous greenhouse. No one answered.

The pale light from the kitchen window snapped off, throwing the lawn between the house and greenhouse into shadow. Corrine was still inside.

"Get a grip, girl. You're tired, that's all." Picking up the trowel, she bent back to the seedlings.

As Linnea scooped the compost mixture for the next pot, the bushes beside the greenhouse door rustled sharply as if pushed aside by a body. She straightened. Her fist tightened around the trowel, and holding it in front of her like a knife she approached the door, placing one foot in front of the other as softly as she could, skirting the light illuminating the tea herbs and keeping to the shadows. As she slid her hand across the knob, the pale light over the tea plants flicked off. The greenhouse was plunged into heavy darkness.

Panic surged through her. *Was this how Marco and Adam felt before the shell tore through their bodies?*

Crack!

A glass pane at the side of the greenhouse splintered. Glass shards pinged against her shoulder and neck, then a heavy object nicked the side of her head. Tiny points of light flashed before her, and her knees buckled, slamming into the concrete floor. Her head caromed off the rubber mat by the door.

A few moments later, the back door of the house banged open.

"Linnea? Are you there? What's going on?" Corrine shouted her name.

Linnea tried to open her mouth, but her jaw didn't work. Pain pounded the back of her skull where she'd hit the floor.

"Linnea! Let me in. I heard glass break." It was Corrine again, this time her voice was accompanied by sharp jabs to Linnea's shoulder. Linnea opened her eyes and twisted her aching head. Her body blocked the door. It hit her shoulder again. She needed to move. Scraping the uninjured side of her head onto the cold cement floor, she cleared space for Corrine. The door banged against her and held. A small wedge of Corrine's face appeared.

"Linnea! Oh my god. You're hurt."

Linnea pressed a hand to the side of her head. It came away sticky with blood. "It's just a scratch. I'll be fine in a minute."

Corrine pulled a cell phone from the pocket of her caftan. "I'm calling Jesse."

"Not Jesse." But she was glad.

"He'll know what to do," Corrine said firmly and punched his number. The conversation was brief and to the point: *Someone threw a rock through the greenhouse and hit Linnea … She's bleeding … We're in the greenhouse … Of course, how stupid of me.*

Corrine turned back to Linnea. "Jesse's coming, and he's calling Teddy. He said to go in the house and lock the doors and call an ambulance for you."

Gingerly, Linnea lifted her head off the floor and propped herself on her elbows. Except for a sharp pain where her head connected with the mat, she seemed to be in one piece. Using the edge of a table, she hoisted herself to her feet and took inventory. Legs, arms, neck, body. Everything in working order. "It's nothing. I don't need an ambulance."

Corrine slipped her hand under Linnea's chin, turned her head gently and inspected the wound. "It's stopped bleeding, but you should go to the hospital just to be safe."

What if Ken got wind of this? He'd be up here to claim her before the doctor slapped a Band-Aid on the side of her head. "I'm fine. Let's get in the house." She shivered. "That guy could still be around."

Although Linnea was perfectly capable of walking on her own, Corrine insisted on helping her into the house. "Sit right here."

Corrine pulled a kitchen chair from the table. "I'll wash out the cut. Let's see, where is my disinfectant?"

The ordinary sounds of running water and bustle as Corrine filled a bowl with soapy water and searched for a clean rag and iodine soothed Linnea's jagged nerves. *She was safe.* She closed her eyes, then they flew open again as the front door burst open.

"Corrine? Lin?"

It was Jesse. At the sound of his voice, relief flooded through Linnea.

"In the kitchen," Corrine called.

A pair of boots clattered across the great room's wood floor, then Jesse filled the kitchen doorway. Linnea turned and met his eyes. They were brimming with concern.

"Are you okay, Lin?" The words flowed over her, velvety and reassuring.

She nodded.

For a long moment his gaze locked into hers. Curiosity, recognition, desire tumbled between them, then he frowned and looked over at Corrine.

"Look at the blood. We should call an ambulance," he said.

Linnea shook her head. "No hospital. I'm fine."

His eyes slid over her body, taking in the streaks of blood on her tee shirt and the yawning hole in her jeans that exposed a dirty, scraped kneecap. "Do you want to wash up before Teddy gets here?" He was all business now, and when he looked at her again, his expression was shuttered. A chill skittered through her. Whatever he'd felt a few moments earlier hadn't been welcome.

A siren wailed in the distance, growing louder as it approached.

"This is all I have to wear."

"It's just family—and Teddy—my nightgown and Robbie's robe will be fine, dear," said Corrine.

What choice did she have? And a shower would clear her head … and wash thoughts of Jesse out of it.

*

Linnea pulled one of Corrine's faded flannel nightgowns over head then rubbed her damp hair with a towel. She turned to the mirror. The girl who stared back looked too young and too vulnerable to handle the huge problems that pressed in on her—helping Adam, avoiding Ken, finding a permanent home. But handle them she would. Must.

A man waited in the half-darkness outside the bathroom. It was Jesse. "Are you sure you're okay, Lin?"

"As good as can be expected."

"If there's anything I can do…." His voice faded away.

Just hold me for a minute. She stepped toward him and pressed herself against his solid chest. His arms slid around her, his palms pressed against her back. The scent of his skin filled her head.

"I'm sorry this happened, Lin. It's my fault for leaving you alone like that."

Her face was buried in his shoulder so she couldn't answer. She didn't want to. It was enough to feel his strength wrap around her like a warm blanket. His arms squeezed her shoulders.

"I want you to pack up your things and go back to Denver first thing tomorrow," he said.

She was not ready to deal with Ken or ready to tear herself away from this wonderful family. "You need me."

"You could have been killed tonight. You're not safe in Cloud River."

"It was a little rock. Besides, Corrine gets lonely at night, and I'm good company. You can ask her."

"That's not the point."

"Don't make me go back yet. I feel like I, uh, haven't paid you back."

He sighed. "We'll talk more about this later. Teddy's waiting in the living room. Are you well enough to answer a few questions?"

She didn't want to face Teddy again. Not after the supermarket and the jail, and her humiliating confession while Jesse watched with a triumphant look on his face. "Can we do it tomorrow?"

He pulled Robbie's old flannel robe from the hook on the bathroom door and held it out to her. "It wasn't a real question. He's not leaving until he sees you."

Teddy was ensconced in the brown easy chair. A jagged half of a brick in a plastic bag sat on the coffee table in front of him. When he saw Linnea, he rose.

"How are you feeling?"

"Okay."

He waved his hand at the sofa. "Please sit down." To Jesse he said, "Can we have a few moments alone?"

A frown knotted the skin between Jesse's brows.

"I need to ask the victim a few questions."

Jesse nodded. "See if you can talk her into leaving Cloud River." Then he strolled into the kitchen where his voice and Corrine's intertwined in soft whispers.

Linnea perched on the edge of the sofa nervously and watched Teddy pull out a smartphone.

"You don't mind if I record this interview, do you?"

She shook her head, but he didn't notice. He was already pressing the app and setting the device on the table between them. She concentrated on the thick freckles and red hair on Teddy's wrists so she wouldn't have to look at him.

"Please state your name."

"Linnea Basinger Reyes."

"Can you tell me what happened this evening around eight o'clock?"

She shrugged. "Not much to tell. I was working in the greenhouse. I heard a rustle in the bushes, and the next thing I know something heavy crashed through the glass and hit the side of my head."

"What were you doing at the time?"

"Transplanting seedlings."

"Corrine said she found you by the door."

"Well, yes, when I heard the rustle, I got a little nervous."

"Why were you nervous?"

"I felt someone watching me, then the rustle. It made me nervous because I wasn't expecting anyone to be outside the greenhouse."

"Why?"

"Jesse and Adam were gone, and Corrine was in the house."

"Did you see anything?"

She shifted uncomfortably. He was heading somewhere with his questions, and she was beginning to see where. "No. It happened just like I told you. Why are you interrogating me?"

"Just a few more questions. I promise. You're doing a great job."

"You think I did this to myself, don't you?"

She raised her head. Teddy's brow arched. "You have a history of dramatics."

The incident in the supermarket automatically made her a prime suspect in this new "drama." Her voice rose. "I explained all that."

Jesse appeared at the kitchen door. "Come on, Teddy. She's not the criminal here." A well of gratitude filled Linnea. He was on her side. Corrine hovered behind him, a hand pressed against her mouth, worry shimmering in her eyes.

"I'm doing my job. That's why I asked both of you to give us some privacy."

Jesse's eyes narrowed. "Go easy on her." Then he spun around and returned to the kitchen with Corrine.

Teddy checked his smart phone. "Let's see, where were we?"

"You were accusing me of hitting myself on the side of the head with a brick."

Across the expanse of coffee table, Teddy studied her. His mouth tightened. "Did you see anything before the brick hit you?"

"No. It knocked me to the ground. Then Corrine came so he must have been gone by then."

"Whoever it was had to know the farm pretty well to disappear so fast."

She was tired, her head ached, and she had no freaking idea how Teddy wanted her to answer. "You're the detective."

"Police officer."

"Sorry." She rubbed her eyes. "I'm really tired."

"Just a few more minutes. You know where I'm going with these questions?"

"Not a clue."

"Why do you think someone would throw this brick at you then run away?"

"A prank?"

"Come on."

Hysteria edged her voice. "I said I don't know."

Jesse—God bless him—stuck his head out of the kitchen. She wanted to run to him, feel his steady, capable arms close around her again. "Everything all right?"

"If we're too loud, I can finish this down at the station," Teddy said tightly.

When Jesse's head disappeared, Teddy shifted forward and lifted the brick. "Did you look closely at the weapon?"

She shook her head. "It's just a brick."

"Maybe." His thick hand turned it over and pushed it close to her. In heavy black marker someone had written *Go Home*.

Chapter Eight

"You must be the bitch who got Jesse arrested." Inches shorter than Linnea—even in spiky heels—the curvaceous woman barreled at her with the ferocity of an angry pit bull.

Fortunately Corrine had a little pit bull in her as well. "Ashley Cooper! You behave yourself." She slid her arm through Linnea's.

Ashley ground to a halt in front of them, barring their way to The Muffin Man. "Well she is." Then she folded her arms over a very expensive-looking red leather jacket and glowered at Linnea.

Linnea shrank a little closer to Corrine. Next to this voluptuous purebred, who wore perfectly tailored black trousers and a silky blouse under her jacket, she felt like a scruffy stray. She lifted her hand and patted the loose braid hanging down her back, then smoothed her fingers down Jess's cast-off khaki tee shirt until she found the hole in her jeans. She held her hand over the tear.

"Linnea is a dear friend. Jesse asked her to stay and help out at the farm," said Corrine.

"Only because you won't do the right thing and because *she*..." Ashley turned her head and glared at Linnea, "screwed everything up so Jesse couldn't go away like he planned."

"As if you would have a clue what the right thing is," said Corrine.

Ashley's mouth, coated in siren-red lipstick, formed a tight line. "You're missing the point."

Corrine didn't even blink. "The point? As far as I can tell, the point is that I'm not as impressed with your money as my son is, and you can't buy me."

Ashley's black-rimmed eyes blazed with anger. "We'll just see about that, won't we?" She spun around and clip-clopped back the way she came. Linnea and Corrine watched her slam into a blue BMW convertible and peel away from the curb.

"Who's that?"

"Ashley Cooper. She's a spoiled brat. Her family owns half the town, but that's not good enough for her. She's got it in her head to buy our farm and pave it over for one of Cooper Homes' ugly subdivisions. I've told her 'no' a dozen times, but she won't listen." Corrine shook her head. "I can't understand what Jesse sees in her."

"Jesse? Is he going out with her?"

"They were an item back in high school. Now she's mostly a convenience for him." Her eyes narrowed. "Although maybe it's the other way around."

"You mean he's sleeping with her?"

"Just a suspicion."

What did he see in that dolled-up witch? Linnea shrugged it off. Jesse McCormick's sex life was none of her business.

Corrine pulled open the door to The Muffin Man and waved Linnea inside. Gleaming glass cases piled high with muffins, Danish, cookies, cupcakes, and layer cakes tempted her. From somewhere in the back of the shop, the smell of vanilla wafted out and hung in the air. A mural depicting a quaint medieval town covered the walls. Narrow, Tudor-style houses and cobblestone streets circled the bakery cases. On one wall a man with a mustache held a tray of muffins and beside him, three children with pennies clutched in their hands waited to choose a muffin.

"The mural is amazing."

"Harry's wife painted it a few years before she passed away. The Muffin Man is Harry when he was younger. The models for the children were their daughter, Hannah and Jesse and Adam." Linnea studied the children more closely. The artist had captured a dark-haired, laughing boy of six or seven holding the hand of a red-haired girl with Pippi Longstocking pigtails. Adam and Hannah. A boy of eleven or twelve stood straight and tall on The Muffin Man's other side. He was nearly identical to the younger boy, but his somber expression as he considered the tray of muffins told her he was as different from his brother as the moon was from the sun. Jesse.

Corrine stared wistfully at the painting. "Adam and Hannah have been inseparable since they were babies. Robbie and I thought they would marry someday. But since Adam's been back home, he's avoided her."

Guilt pricked at Linnea. "I'm sorry."

"Corrine!" The mustached man from the supermarket poked his head out of the kitchen in the back. He wore a starched white apron and a paper cap.

"Harry!"

Harry came around the counter and gave Corrine a big hug. "I heard about the attack last night. Are you okay?"

"I was in the house when it happened. Linnea's the one who got hit with a brick."

"Why would anyone do such a terrible thing?"

"A lot of crazy, hateful people in the world," said Corrine. "Jesse wants Linnea to go back to Denver, but our girl won't be scared off that easily."

"So he gave me the morning off instead," Linnea said to hide her embarrassment. It was cowardice not bravery keeping her in Cloud River. She wasn't ready to have it out with Ken. She grabbed a fistful of her borrowed tee shirt. "Besides, I want to buy some clothes that fit." Maybe Jesse would stay home at night if she looked like a normal girl.

Harry reached out and patted their shoulders. "I'm glad you're both safe. Let me get you some muffins. On the house."

A pretty girl in an apron and paper cap like Harry's stuck her head out of the kitchen. A dusting of flour streaked across her freckled forehead, and blue eyes twinkled brightly. Beneath her cap, red curls corkscrewed around her head.

She hugged Corrine before turning to Linnea. "I'm Hannah. Harry's daughter."

"And partner," Harry added proudly.

Hannah rolled her eyes, but she looked pleased and proud. "Just call me the Queen of Tarts." They all laughed. Hannah turned back to Corrine. "How's Adam doing? We don't see him around much."

"Between school and the radio station, he's pretty busy."

"Yeah." Hannah sounded disappointed. "Well, if the station ever gives him a Saturday night off, tell him to call me. Maybe we can grab something to eat and catch up."

Corrine patted her shoulder. "Of course, dear. I'll give him the message."

For a moment, Hannah looked sad, then she seemed to gather herself together. "Well I better get back to work."

As soon as she disappeared, Harry scooted behind the counter. "Pick any muffin you like, ladies."

Linnea survey the towers of muffins stacked on antique cake stands. Her head spun from all the mouth-watering choices. There were the traditional muffins like blueberry, bran raisin, and cinnamon-swirl, but Harry had unique combinations too, including orange cranberry, chocolate chip raspberry, and lemon-lime. She studied the muffins as Corrine and Harry's chatter swirled around her like soft music.

"How's business?"

"Not bad, Corrine." Harry pulled open the sliding door on one of the cases. "Bran raisin. Right?"

Corrine nodded.

"With the brewery going gang-busters and the new art gallery at the corner, there's more foot traffic," he said. "Next month a bookstore is opening around the corner, and I heard someone just applied for a permit for a vintage clothing store. People are coming from all over to shop."

"What about the mall?"

"We got over two thousand signatures on our petition. The council meeting is next month. You'll be there, won't you?"

"Of course. Adam has been talking about it every night and keeping the phone lines open. Most of the callers are expressing opposition. I hope the city council is listening."

Harry shook his head. "Cloud River has always been a town of peace and brotherhood. A haven to all of us refugees from modern civilization. It's sad to think its future hangs by a thread."

He sighed and turned to Linnea. "What can I get you, young lady?"

"They all look so good. Pick something for me, please."

He studied her. "After seeing your performance the other day at the supermarket, a spicy cinnamon-swirl would suit you. Never thought I'd see the day when a gal would get the best of Jesse McCormick. What did that son-of-a-gun do? Break your heart?"

Linnea blushed. "Not exactly."

Corrine came to her rescue again. "Can you wrap up the muffins, Harry? We have to go."

"Sure thing, Corrine. I'll put two extra in the bag for the boys. Let's see." He surveyed the case. "The orange cranberry is for Adam." He lifted his head out of the case and winked at Linnea. "If he likes it, he'll say something on his radio show. Give me some free advertising." He bent and pulled out a blueberry muffin. "Jess always has the blueberry. That one's the traditionalist. If I didn't know better, I'd swear someone left him on Robbie and Corrine's doorstep."

Corrine pretended to be shocked, but the corners of her mouth were turned upward. They all laughed, Linnea the loudest. It felt good to laugh.

It was noon when Linnea and Corrine returned from their shopping trip. Linnea scurried into Corrine's bedroom to change into her new jeans and a fitted, scoop-neck green tee shirt that

Corrine said brought out the color of her eyes. She slipped a pair of bright silver hoops into her ears and surveyed the results in the mirror. The image reflected back at her didn't look quite so forlorn.

Her step was light as she skirted a flock of brass children in the living room and ducked under a gigantic macramé web. In the kitchen Corrine was stacking a plate with turkey sandwiches for Jesse's lunch.

"I'll take them," said Linnea. "I'm going back to work."

"No lunch?"

Linnea patted her belly. "That muffin did me in. Maybe I'll grab something later."

Corrine nodded, but the gleam in her eyes said she knew what Linnea was thinking. "Go on then. Show Jesse your new clothes."

"I don't care what—"

"Hush. Don't tell me what I know." Corrine handed Linnea the sandwiches and a thermos of tea and waved her out the door.

Jesse was harvesting bean sprouts, lifting mossy bunches of bright green from long plastic trays with an oversized fork and draining them before he transferred them to a scale. When he saw Linnea, he straightened up and gave an enthusiastic wolf whistle.

She shot him a withering look, but it pleased her that he liked her new clothes. She handed over his lunch and took his place in front of the trays. She lifted a bunch of the sprouts with the fork, draining the excess water off before setting them on the scale and packaging them into three-ounce bundles. Jesse pulled one of Corrine's campstools close and sat down to eat. He ate the first sandwich in a few bites, then poured tea from the thermos into the metal cap. He gulped the tea down and picked up his second sandwich. He bit into it as he watched her work.

"It would go a lot faster—"

"I know. It would go a lot faster if I did it in a factory line." She smiled at him. "It's more fun this way."

He tilted his head and studied her thoughtfully as he chewed. "So tell me, how did you end up working for Senator Klein?"

She brushed an invisible speck of dirt off the scale. "The usual way."

"Really? Would that be sexy intern or big contributor?"

Her head snapped up, and she stared at him. What had he guessed? One dark brow arched, the gold sparks in his eyes glittered with challenge. She struggled to catch a breath so her answer would roll off her tongue smoothly. "You're being dramatic. It's much more boring."

He took another bite of his sandwich. "Tell me. I promise not to yawn."

Except for the soft splash of water dripping off the sprouts, the greenhouse was silent. Bright sunshine streamed through the roof. She fiddled with a little bundle of sprouts while she sorted out her story.

"Well, okay then." She cleared her throat. "I've actually known Ken since I was little. We lived in Grand Junction and my mother was the Klein's nanny. His family owned mines and land there. Then Ken got a divorce and moved to Denver to go into politics. His kids were getting old, so we followed him. My mother kept his house and paid his bills, managed his appointments. Stuff like that." She hesitated.

"And?"

"And then she died." Linnea lifted a forkful of sprouts from the bin and watched them drain.

"I'm sorry."

"Don't be. It happened a million years ago."

"A million?" He set his half-eaten sandwich back on the plate.

"Ten. Almost."

"Your father?"

She spun on him. "Look, Jesse, I—"

"Tell me." It was a command.

"I don't have one. My mother never said who he was. Never told anyone."

"I see. So the Senator took you under his wing."

He didn't seem to care that she was a fatherless bastard. Her body relaxed. "Not exactly. I married my high school boyfriend and we moved in with his family. After a few years, he joined the army, and so I worked as a nanny like my mom and paid my way through college. When Marco died, I couldn't stay with his mom and stuff, so Ken gave me a job on his campaign and let me stay in one of the apartments he keeps for his DC staff. Because of my mother and everything." This version sounded so much better than "my husband joined the army because he was sick of being married to me, and Ken expects payback for his favors."

"You've had it kinda rough, haven't you?"

She kept her face very still. "I can take care of myself."

He studied her again, sympathy filling his eyes, his sandwich forgotten, the sprouts clinging to the fork in her hand long past dry. The silence between them grew.

Why was he acting like this was a big deal? None of it *mattered.* But how could she expect him to understand? He'd had a mother and a father, a home, love. She was an interesting specimen to regular people like Jesse. Linnea forced a casual smile to her lips. "Hey, finish your lunch. We got work to do."

He reached out and picked up his sandwich without glancing away from her. If he didn't stop staring, she would end up telling him everything. She tried to distract him.

"Your turn. Why don't you and Adam call your mom and dad, 'mom and dad'?"

He took a bite of his sandwich. "There's more to your story than you're telling me."

"That's it. Honest. Little Orphan Annie goes to college. And here I am." She spread her arms and curtsied. "You didn't answer my question."

He stuffed the last bite of his sandwich in his mouth and stood up. "My parents didn't believe in labels and forcing children into social roles." He took a step toward her. He was so close, the warmth of his body seeped through her tee shirt.

She fought for control of the conversation. "So if I ever want to raise free spirits, I should send my children to a military academy." She tried to smile at her joke, but it faded before it reached her lips. His mouth hovered over hers. What would feel like to kiss him?

"Tell me the rest."

She chose her most innocent secret. "Marco—my husband—didn't want to be married to me anymore. That's why he joined up. After Marco died, his mother blamed me."

"Was there another woman?"

Her face began to burn. "Yes."

He hesitated. "Did you love him?"

His warm breath fluttered against her mouth. The truth floated across her tongue. "He was all I had."

He touched her lips with his. The barest brush of a kiss. Her nerve endings sputtered to life, and she stifled the urge to press herself against him.

"That wasn't so hard, was it?" he asked.

"What do you mean?"

He took a step back from her. "As Corrine puts it, you have trust issues. Fair enough, considering. But I can't figure out if that's turned you into a teller of tales or a keeper of secrets."

She picked up the fork and began to drain sprouts again. She couldn't look at him. "Aren't they flip sides of the same coin?"

His deep voice held a warning. "Maybe, Lin. Maybe not."

*

"Where are you?"

Watching Jesse's van disappear over the lip in the road with a load of sprouts for the Cloud River Supermarket. But she couldn't exactly say that to her boss. "Ken?"

"Of course. Where are you?"

"I met some friends on my way back to Denver, and they invited me to stay for awhile."

"What about your job?"

"I'll have a story before the deadline." She rolled her eyes. She was going to have to figure something out fast.

There was a long pause. "This is about what happened in the limo, isn't it?"

Her heart began to pound. "Limo? Oh, that." She took a gulp of air. "Don't be ridiculous."

"Look, I got a little carried away, and the car hit a bump. If I frightened you, I apologize."

"I'd forgotten all about it." *Liar.*

Ken sighed theatrically. "You're going to have to return to Denver eventually. When you do, we'll sit down and have a long talk. Sort everything out."

With sixty-five miles separating them, it would be safer to speak her mind now. "That's fine, Ken, but just so you know, I'm not interested in you that way."

"Linnea, Linnea." He sounded as if he were speaking to a stubborn child. "You're getting ahead of yourself. We'll talk face to face. Then you can decide."

"I won't change my mind."

"Linnea." She could almost hear his jaw tighten. "I don't want to argue with you over the phone."

"Ken—"

"Good night. I expect to see you at your desk, eight o'clock sharp on Monday morning. Do you understand?" The line went dead.

Linnea stared out at the distant mountains and felt the day's warmth and peace drain away. It was Thursday afternoon. She had exactly three days and four nights to figure out her next move.

Chapter Nine

Jesse glanced at the moon-faced clock hanging in the supermarket's back room. Ten thirteen. It felt like midnight to his exhausted body. He'd told Lin that he was going to the bar again tonight because the truth made him look weak and pathetic. He needed this job.

He rose from his chair, stretched, and strolled to the kitchenette for coffee. Pulling a Styrofoam cup from the stack beside the coffee pot, he poured another cup of the acrid-tasting brew. Then he crammed his long legs under the desk again and tried to focus on the ledger glaring at him from the computer screen.

Could his life get any worse? He was sitting in the same cramped office in the same run-down supermarket where he spent his evenings back in high school and summers during college, straightening out ledgers that would just go back to being hopelessly screwed up the minute he left.

How did a graduate of West Point and an ex-army officer with more than twenty thousand hours of flight time end up laboring eighteen hours a day and barely making the minimum wage if you counted the abysmal income on the organics? He grimaced and bent his head to the computer screen.

A set of light knuckles rapped on the back door. "Jess? Open up. It's me. Ash."

Jesse closed his eyes. Another woman who wanted something from him.

She rapped on the door again. "Come on, Jesse. I saw the van in the parking lot. I know you're in there."

He stood up. God, how his back muscles ached. Some mornings he felt a thousand years old. He put his hands on his hips and arched his spine, trying to straighten out the kinks.

"I mean it. I'm not leaving until you let me in. I have to talk to you."

"I'm coming." Then he yanked open the door before she got pissy. She wore her kitty-cat outfit tonight—tight black jeans tucked into black boots with heels that reminded him of daggers and her white fur jacket. The fur hung open giving him a fantastic aerial view of generous breasts tucked into a tight black tank.

She batted her eyes at him. "I was driving by and saw your van. I just had to stop."

Jesse stood back and waved her in. Then he shut the door and locked it again.

Ashley surveyed the room. His eyes followed hers as they trailed over the cheap desk with strips of veneer curling off the sides, past rows of blue smocks to the dingy green kitchen counter holding an industrial coffee maker and a scattering of cups with congealed creamer floating on cold coffee. Dog-eared gossip magazines were piled up on a cheap dinette table beside a half-dozen pink napkins slumped in an acrylic napkin holder.

She sighed. "Boy, if this room could talk." Her hand spider-walked up Jesse's arm. "Remember when I'd sneak out after my parents were asleep, and you'd be in here working, and we'd—"

"I remember." He pulled his arm away.

She eyed the table. "Wouldn't it be a blast to do it here for old time's sake?" She took a step closer to him, slid her arms around his waist, and tipped her head up to him. She blinked at him, her lashes fluttering like black widow spiders caught in a wind storm.

Had he fallen so low he'd screw his high school girlfriend in the back of a supermarket? Adrienne, his beautiful, long-legged lady flashed across his brain. They'd begun to talk about marriage, and between his own service record and her father being a four-star general, his promotion to captain seemed certain. The life he always dreamed of lay before him like a banquet. Then his father got cancer and Adam lost his leg, but Adrienne refused to cut him any slack.

Do you love me or your family?

What kind of officer, or man for that matter, turns his back on his family?

What about us? What about your promotion?

I can't walk away from my personal responsibilities.

I hate you. Get out.

Though a year had passed, the argument ran through his head at least a dozen times a day. He couldn't seem to let it go.

Jesse tipped his head down for one last longing gander at the lovely mounds pressed against his chest. "I've got a lot of work to do."

"Whatever. You have to come over to my place later. You owe me."

"Owe you?"

"It cost me a thousand bucks to get you out of jail."

"You got your money back. Besides, by the time you showed up, it was too late to make it to Winter Park."

Ashley's red lips curled into a kittenish pout. "I don't have that much cash just lying around." Her hands slid around his waist and over his ass.

"The tires on your car cost a thousand dollars. Hell, that white thing you're wearing probably cost five times my bail money."

Ashley blinked at him. "As if Teddy would let me use it for bail. None of this is my fault, you know. It's that stupid bitch who set you up." She rubbed her hips against his. "She looks like a bag lady."

"You saw her?"

"She was in town with your mother this morning. Her clothes were all holey and baggy and gross. She didn't even have lipstick on."

Lin's lips had tasted sweet when they brushed against his. She didn't need lipstick. "Did you say anything to her?"

"Well of course I did. Then your mother got all rude and huffy about it. But it was just the truth. She's a bitch."

Jesse untwined her arms from his waist. "She's not a bitch. Corrine's right. You were out of line."

"Why are you mad at me? Look around you. You're sitting in this stupid supermarket in the middle of the night because of *her*. I was trying to defend you." She studied him, a sly look lighting her eyes. "Who is she anyway? Where did she come from? No one in town seems to know."

"Just an old friend."

"I don't believe you."

He studied her unhappy face. Whatever he told her would be all over town by tomorrow. An image popped into his head of Lin emerging from the bathroom wearing Corrine's granny nightgown buttoned up to her neck. A surge of protectiveness mixed with desire flowed through him. When she fell into his arms, he'd wanted to lift the hem of her nightgown and cup his hands around her bottom.

He forced himself back to the present. Taking Ashley's shoulders, he turned her toward the door. "It's none of your business. Go home."

She spun on him. "You know what? You deserve every stupid thing she did to you. I liked you better when you were in jail. At least you appreciated me a little." Her eyes narrowed. "I hope she does it again because I'm going to come and visit you just to say, 'I told you so.'" She flounced to the door and pulled on it. It didn't budge. "Dammit!"

"It's locked."

"I know!" She flicked the button under the knob and yanked open the door. Then she stopped. "May first, Jess, if you want a decent price for that pile of shit you live in." Then she slammed the door behind her.

He stood for a few minutes staring at nothing, listening to her car roar to life and squeal out of the parking lot. He wasn't going to see her bedroom for awhile, and he didn't really care.

Jesse turned back to the desk. The computer screen flickered at him, its low, steady buzz vibrating against every hard surface in the room. He'd left his iPod at home, but maybe the drip of the coffee maker would drown out the silence. As he scooped the grounds into a filter-lined basket, Lin popped back into his thoughts.

Working in the greenhouse wasn't as dull with her at his side. The first day, when she'd appeared wearing Corrine's rubber boots and one of his khaki tee shirts, her blond hair pulled back in a ponytail, she looked like the kid sister he never had. But whenever he glanced over at her, his eyes seemed to fall on the long column of her neck and the soft swell of a breast, reminding him that she was a grown woman and not his sister at all.

He pushed the basket of grounds into the coffeemaker, pressed the "on" button and went back to the desk.

And she had grown-up problems that were none of his business. The last thing he needed was get involved with Lin. First of all, he had plenty of his own problems without taking on whatever ghosts were haunting her. But more importantly, he wanted his freedom back. He would do two years with Keystone then either re-up with the army or find a job with lots of travel. No more relationships. Adrienne had taught him how trivial and fleeting love truly was—a lesson he would never forget.

When he got back on his feet, he would have a woman waiting in every city he frequented, and he didn't care if they knew about each other. In fact, that would be preferable. It meant they were willing to play by his new rules of engagement.

*

Ring. Ring. Ring. Jesse opened an eye. White Styrofoam cup at eye level. He was still in the supermarket. He'd been asleep. For a second, his cheek stuck to the veneer when he lifted his head off the desk. *Ring. Ring. Ring.*

His cell's rotary phone ring tone boomeranged against the wall in the silent office. His hands curled around the phone's smooth casing, and he checked the caller I.D. His heart skipped a beat. It was Glenn Keystone.

"Hey, Glenn."

"Did I wake you?"

Jesse glanced up at the clock. One forty-five. "Nah." He rubbed the side of his face that had rested on the desk. It felt stiff and hot.

"Good. I'm back in the States. A family emergency came up—nothing serious—so I came home early."

Relief flooded Jesse's body. "That's good to hear. Any chance you got time to meet with me?"

"That's why I'm calling. One of my pilots in Nigeria had a little accident. I'm looking for a replacement. Are you interested?"

Interested? He was ecstatic! A tour in Africa meant top pay and a double-scale signing bonus. "Absolutely. Just tell me where and when."

"Brilliant. I'll be flying my kids up to our place in Winter Park for spring break. That's two weeks from now. Can you be ready to leave for Abuja immediately after we meet? That's the capital. There's been some unrest around the Kaduna refineries just south of there. We need another pilot on the team ASAP."

Jesse stood up and began to pace around the cramped office. Adrenaline pumped through his body in huge waves at this second chance. "Sure."

"Same drill as before. Bring your documents. Passport, discharge papers, medical records."

"No problem." He reached the counter and pivoted. Then he stopped as Keystone cleared his throat. Jesse held his breath.

"There are not going to be any fuck-ups this time, are there?"

"You have my word. I'll see you in two weeks."

"I need to know the men I'm putting on the ground are reliable. You were highly recommended, but I've been successful by going on my own instincts. Get where I'm going with this?"

"Yes."

"Good." The line went dead.

Jesse dropped his phone on the desk and let out a long breath. There'd be no third chance. He didn't need one. This time, he would be at the meeting, because this time he wasn't telling Corrine and Adam until he was back home with a signed contract and a fat check.

There was someone else determined to keep him in Cloud River, too. His hands clenched into tight fists. He couldn't afford to screw up again. It was time for her to go home.

Chapter Ten

Slouched in his favorite spot on the living room couch, Jesse watched the Colorado Rockies skirmish with the Chicago Cubs in spring training. Damn, but he was exhausted. Even with Lin's help, the loss of Kevin Burke's muscle had doubled his workload. Like an idiot, he'd even driven out to Burke's place yesterday to beg Kevin to come back. The son of a bitch was already working for frickin' Cooper Homes—like everyone else in Cloud River—and getting a full night's sleep while he got by on four hours of shut-eye, max. But he'd made it to Saturday. Tonight he was going to recharge his batteries in front of the TV.

"What do you think?"

He unglued his eyes from the game. His mother was twirling across the room like a school girl. Dark slacks hugged her thin body, and a filmy blouse with ruffles around the neck floated around her as she spun. Was he hallucinating or was Corrine wearing gold sandals with a genuine high heel? Her mane of hippie hair was twisted up at the back of her neck, and a pair of chopsticks poked out the top of her bun like a TV antenna. Her cheeks flushed with excitement. Her eyes sparkled. Behind her, Lin looked on like an adoring mother on prom night.

His body surged off the chair. "You look ... I don't know ..."

"Beautiful?" prompted Lin.

"Yeah. Beautiful. Wow." He didn't know what to say.

"Linnea talked me into buying a few things when we went shopping."

"I can see." His gaze slid to Lin's face.

She looked uncertain. "I hope that's okay."

"Of course. I'm just surprised, that's all." He tried to pull himself together. "Is there a reason you're all dolled up tonight?"

As she blushed, Corrine reminded him of the young mother of his childhood. The circles under her eyes had vanished, and her face appeared plumper. His eyes slid back to Lin again. Was this her doing? The idea depressed him. How was he going to get her out of Cloud River and back to Denver when his mother's affection for her—his heart clutched; *dependence*—grew by the day?

"I'm meeting Harry at the Civic Center in Greeley. They're putting on a Woody Guthrie retrospective tonight."

"Harry asked you out?"

She turned to Lin, and they shared a conspiratorial smile. "Actually I asked him out. Just as a friend." The meatloaf from dinner soured in Jesse's stomach.

"My god! Angelina Jolie is standing in our very own living room!" Adam emerged from his bedroom.

"Don't be silly." But her eyes sparkled.

Adam kissed Corrine's cheek. "My deepest apologies. You are way more awesome than Angelina."

She tapped his arm playfully. "How did I raise such a terrible flirt?" Then her eyes swept past Jesse and back to Lin. Lin nodded encouragingly. "Well, I better go. I don't want to keep Harry waiting."

Adam extended his arm. "As I am off to my gig at the station, I insist on escorting you out to the van, m'lady."

Head held high, Corrine slid her arm through Adam's, and the two sashayed to the door. Corrine's delicate hips swayed from side to side, and Adam's limp was barely noticeable. Jesse felt the stab of an unfamiliar emotion. Optimism?

Adam bowed theatrically as he opened the door for Corrine. "Do I detect a little romance in the air?"

"You detect a little friendship in the air," retorted Corrine.

Then the door closed behind them, and he was alone with Lin. A night unencumbered by the watchful presence of Corrine or Adam stretched before them. An opportunity to dislodge Miss

Alice from their lives if he could figure out exactly how to do it without looking like a jerk. He studied her.

She folded her arms across her chest and met his gaze straight on. "Going out for a beer tonight?"

Maybe a drink would soften her mood and make her more receptive to returning home. He dropped onto the sofa, popped his feet on the coffee table and gave her his most charming smile. "Thought I might." She glared at him. "Care to join me?"

Her eyes widened with surprise. "Me? Yes. I'd love to." She shot him a sunny smile that tore through him. "Thanks."

The meatloaf roiled in his stomach.

She surveyed her dirty tee shirt and jeans, and her face fell. "Do I have time to wash up a little?"

"Take all the time you want." He needed to grab a handful of antacid tablets and pull himself together. "Things don't get started for the under-fifty crowd quite this early. Besides I have to jump in the shower."

"All right, then. I'll see you in a little while."

He watched her half-skip, half-run from the room and felt like an asshole. His invitation to a kiss-off had turned into a date.

An hour later, showered and shaved, his rebellious stomach under control, he strolled into the living room prepared to deal with his nemesis. She'd changed into a denim skirt and her green tee shirt, which clung to her tall, slender body in all the right places. Corrine's white shawl entwined her arms. Her hair was loose, reminding him of a gleaming honey-gold veil. His fingers itched to touch it.

She tilted her head and attempted a rueful smile. "Do I look okay?"

He wanted to press his lips against the base of her throat. Instead he channeled Adam. "I am surrounded by beauty tonight."

A pink stain spread across her cheeks. "You don't have to flatter me."

He'd sooner give up his silver star than wipe that sweet look from her face, but what choice did he have? "I'm not. Come on, let's go."

Her eyes narrowed, but she followed him.

Carless and van-less, he drove her Silverado. The radio played U2's *One*. She tapped her foot softly to the music. How to begin? He glanced over at her. Goose bumps peppered her arms. "Cold?"

"Maybe a little."

He turned up the heat.

The memory of Corrine, flushed and excited flashed in his head. "How are you and Corrine getting along?"

"Okay, I guess."

"Is she keeping you up at night?"

"Not really. She has a little trouble falling asleep, but once she's asleep, she out until morning."

He waited for her to say more, but she shifted in her seat and adjusted one of the vents in the dashboard. Her foot tapped away as Bono belted out lyrics. He tried working a lighter vein. "No snoring?"

She tossed back her head and laughed. Her hair floated over her shoulders. He felt a small stab of triumph. "Absolutely not." She turned away from him and stared out at the passing houses and fields through the passenger window.

"I hear you two talking at night sometimes." Lin twisted around in her seat and studied him. "I was just wondering what you were whispering about." More to the point, was Corrine going to be devastated when Lin left?

She propped her elbow on the back of the seat and continued her inspection. He squirmed.

"Well, she likes to talk about your dad for one thing. I've heard some great stories about when they met and first came to Cloud River. Um, let's see. She told me about her uncle who made a fortune manufacturing tents for the Korean War then built your house and devoted his life to organic farming and supporting starving artists.

"She's told me some funny stuff about you and Adam when you were little." Linnea hesitated.

"Go on."

"She worries about you and Adam a lot." Her words drove into him like a punch in the gut. He felt naked and humiliated. And pissed.

"Really." Flipping the signal, he turned into the highway and concentrated on the merging traffic so she couldn't see the outrage that stiffened his face.

"Especially you." Lin spoke the words softly. "She knows you made a big sacrifice for her, and she's afraid she ruined your life."

How dare she—this stranger—explain his mother's feelings to him? "In case you haven't noticed my mother overreacts to everything."

He felt her stiffen beside him. "In case *you* haven't noticed, she has a lot of reasons to."

"What makes you think you know more about my mother than I do?" The words ground against his teeth.

"Because I know how to listen."

"What the hell is that supposed to mean?" He roared the words, and his voice bounced back at him from the dashboard and vibrated in his ears.

In a raspy, condescending whisper, she came right back at him. "I'll tell you what that means, Jesse. It means that you always think you're right, and no one could possibly have anything important to teach you, least of all your mother."

"You're crazy."

That did it. "Maybe I am, but you bark orders at your family like they were your foot soldiers. Left, right, left. Stay in line. Follow orders. That's you."

Was it? He didn't mean to be harsh with Corrine and Adam. He just wanted them to be safe, that's all. But even if a little of what she said was true, it was definitely not her place to point it out to him. "You are way over the line, lady. This is private family business."

Her face fell. The fire in her eyes died away, replaced by the dull glimmer of hurt.

He forced himself to relax. But he was boiling mad. If she wasn't a girl, he'd stop the truck right now and have it out, man to man, fist to fist.

She twisted back in her seat and folded her arms across her chest. "Take me home."

Home? His anger drained away, replaced by shock. She'd just referred to the house he planned to sell to Ashley Cooper for demolition as "home." This evening was off the rails. He tried to pull it back on the track. "Look, Lin, I'm sorry. I didn't mean to sound so…" He trailed off.

She generously chipped in the next word. "Nasty?"

He swallowed his pride. "Yeah. Sorry." He attempted a lopsided, boyish grin. "Still up for that drink?"

She studied him for a few moments, her gaze narrow and unfriendly. "I don't know." He took that as a sign of encouragement.

"I know I've been tough to be around lately, but I promise to do better, starting tonight."

She rolled her eyes.

"Can I get a second chance? Please."

The golden word seemed to do the job. Her face softened, and he knew he had her. "Whatever," she said and turned away.

*

Linnea sank back into the Silverado's passenger seat and closed her eyes. She'd drunk two rum and colas at the brewery but instead of escaping her worries, she had a pounding headache, plus she was one day closer to Monday when Ken expected her back in Denver "to talk."

"Are you okay?"

Or maybe it wasn't the rum and colas making her head pound. Maybe her problem was sitting beside her in the truck. She didn't open her eyes. "I'm a little tired."

Just as the enormity of her Ken problem threatened to engulf her, Jesse had apparently launched a campaign to drive her out of Cloud River. Like a stupid idiot, she assumed he invited her out for a drink because he liked her. While she dressed tonight, she'd thought about the soft kiss he'd given her in the greenhouse. Would he kiss her again?

But his invitation had been straight business. As soon as they were settled at a table with their drinks, his bare-knuckle approach to dealing with every problem hit her square between her naïve eyes. *We're really going to miss you when you leave. By the way, when do you think you'll be heading back to Denver?* He was about as subtle as a jackhammer. She couldn't deal with him, not with Ken breathing down her neck, so she'd engrossed herself in the Rockies v Cubs game on the big screen over the bar and ignored him.

He took a right out of the parking lot. Once the truck was humming along the blacktop, he cleared his throat. Her heart sank. He was going to talk again.

"You really seem to know a lot about the Cubs. For a Colorado girl, I mean."

"My mother was a Cubs fan." When he didn't respond, she sighed and added, "I grew up watching the games with her." *Leave me alone.*

"Seems odd."

She opened her eyes and sat up. Despite his insufferable behavior tonight, he evidently expected her to chat with him on the drive home. "Does it?"

"Yeah, I mean, why a Chicago team?"

"I have no idea." She crossed her arms and glared at the front windshield. Just ahead a traffic light turned red, and Jesse hit the brakes.

His warm, slightly beer-y breath puffed against her cheek. Shit. He was going to talk again.

"Look, Lin, we got off to a bad start tonight, and I blame myself."

"Good for you."

"I mean it."

She twisted in her seat and faced him. His grin had vanished. "If you have something to say, just say it."

"You can't stay with us much longer. This isn't your life, and I worry that Corrine is becoming dependent on you. I was out of line to make you to stay in the first place. If you'd been seriously hurt the other night, I'd have blamed myself for blackmailing you to stay with us."

She forced herself to smile. "I see."

A truck roared up behind the Silverado, and the driver leaned on the horn. Startled, she jerked her gaze from Jesse. The traffic light glowed green. The driver laid on the horn again and switched on his brights, filling the cab with blinding white light.

Jesse slid the truck into the intersection. "Go around us if you're in such a damn hurry."

The driver stayed on the horn until Linnea's head was ready to split in half. Finally Jesse got the truck up to the speed limit, and the blare of the other truck's horn died away. But the driver stayed right on their bumper, its high-beams flooding the cab.

Jesse glanced back. "What the hell? Can you see who's driving that pickup?"

She craned her neck past the headrest. The white light stung her eyes. "It's too bright."

"Turn around and hang on."

She settled in her seat, and he yanked the Silverado to the left, squealing into a quiet side street of homes. The cab of the Silverado was plunged in soothing darkness, then filled with blinding light again. Their pursuer was right behind them. Jesse picked up speed, careening past the parked mini-vans and economy cars that lined the curb. Through the lighted windows of ranches and split-levels, people reclined in front of TVs. At one house, an angry man ran out his front door, shouting and shaking his fist at them as they roared past.

"Why is he chasing us?"

"I don't know, but we have to get out of this neighborhood before someone gets hurt. I didn't expect him to follow us."

They passed a trim little ranch with a fountain in front. A woman stared out the front window, her eyes wide with alarm. Jesse lurched around a corner, throwing Linnea against the passenger door. The right front and back wheels of the Silverado lifted off the ground. She screamed and hid her face in her hands.

Jesse's voice was cool and reassuring. "Just hang on, Lin. There's an office park past the next intersection. I know the layout. We'll lose this dirt bag in there if he's still on our tail."

She dropped her hands to her lap and tried to act calm. "I'll be fine."

"Good girl."

He jerked the wheel again, and a major intersection came into view. Their pursuer rounded the corner inches from the Silverado's bumper. Up ahead, the traffic light glowed red, and a car waited. Two cars on the cross street turned and drove toward them.

"Shit." Jesse muttered the word under his breath. He laid on the horn and flashed his headlights. The car waiting at the traffic light didn't move.

Linnea started to pray. *Please, God. Help us.*

The Silverado raced past houses and trees, taking each block in just a few blinding seconds. She counted the streets to the intersection as she prayed. Five blocks. Four. *Please.* Three. *I'm sorry, God. I'll make it up to Adam. I promise.* Two.

The other driver leaned on his horn, then rammed the Silverado.

Linnea's head slammed against the headrest. "What are we going to do?" The words emerged on breathy puffs. Her lungs had frozen.

"Stay with me, baby. We're going to make it."

They were close enough to the car at the light that she could see it was a gray Taurus with a rusty bumper. Jesse flashed his lights again. It didn't move. They were less than a block away now, the pickup still riding their bumper when the light finally—mercifully—changed and the car's brake lights flicked off. As it pulled away, Linnea breathed again, then clutched the door handle as Jesse roared into the intersection and squealed left. The pickup stayed with them.

They raced over the deserted street past a lighted sign, "Cloud River Office Park—The Wave of the Future." The Silverado, with it pursuer mere inches from its bumper, roared into the deserted park.

"What are we going to do now?"

Jesse's forehead creased with concentration. He stared out the front windshield, hands tight on the wheel, body hunched over. "We are going to lose this asshole." He pressed his foot on the gas pedal, and the Silverado's engine thundered beneath them.

Linnea's lungs were like lead again. "I can't breathe."

"You have to hold on a little longer. Okay?"

She lifted her hands and pressed them to her chest to still her pounding heart. Her fingers felt numb.

"Here we go."

Jesse pushed the gas pedal to the floor. She jerked backward as the Silverado flew forward. The buildings blurred as they sped past them. The other driver accelerated, too. It charged up behind them, horn blaring, blinding brights filling the Silverado. The clank of metal on metal pierced the air as their pursuer rammed the Silverado's bumper again. Linnea's head smashed a second time against the headrest, and her teeth clicked together. The taste of blood filled her mouth.

"I bit my tongue."

"Stay with me, Lin." It sounded like a command. His tone softened. "We're almost there."

She nodded, slid her fingers around the door handle again, and squeezed. Ahead, the road branched into two streets. Jesse pulled the Silverado toward the left, then just as they reached the junction, he jerked the truck to the right, and the pickup roared to the left. The Silverado raced up the right.

"Can we hide before he turns around?"

"No." Jesse's mouth was a tight line, his body pressed into the steering wheel, his eyes glittering as they flew from windshield to side mirror to rearview mirror and back to windshield again.

He liked this. Linnea grimaced. Well, he was a soldier and a chopper pilot. This was probably all in a day's work when he served in Afghanistan.

Jesse spun left into a narrow alley, then veered left again onto the street their attacker had taken. The Silverado's headlights bounced as they rolled over a speed bump, illuminating the pickup as it made a u-turn.

"Gotcha." Jesse punched the gas pedal and closed in on their attacker.

Her life passed before her eyes. "What are you doing? What if there's more than one guy? What if they have guns?"

"I need a license number."

Her breath sounded like sharp barks. "I ... I can't—"

He reached across the seat and squeezed her knee. His palm was warm. "Come on, Lin. Just another minute. You've been so brave."

His hand griped the wheel again, and the Silverado lurched forward. He flipped on the brights and pressed the heel of his hand to the horn. The other truck accelerated but not fast enough, and Jesse closed the distance between them.

The mystery truck was a shiny red Dodge Ram. The reflective surface of a Colorado license plate flashed at them, its digits standing out in sharp relief. Their headlights limned a single male driver.

Jesse eyes sparkled. "I can take this guy."

"No." *Sob.* "Fighting." *Sob.* "Please."

His exuberance died away. "Yeah. Probably not a good idea." But he didn't sound convinced.

The Silverado slowed, and the pickup roared off into the night. Jesse pulled over and parked.

"Are you all right?"

She shook her head. Her chest heaved, and she struggled to pull air into her lungs. Black spots danced before her eyes. Her hand reached toward him and clutched at his arm.

"It's okay, baby. You're just a little freaked out." He loosened her seatbelt and lowered the windows. Cool air surged through the cab. "Just relax. Breathe in. There. That's better."

She drew in fresh air and felt her chest expand.

"Put your head down. Don't forget to breathe." He pressed the back of her neck gently until her forehead rested on her knees. Then his hand rubbed her back in long, easy strokes until sensation flowed back into her limbs and her lungs pulled in air at regular intervals.

She lifted her head and sank against the seat. Jesse propped a shoulder against the driver's seat and studied her.

His thoughts were so obvious a child could have read them. But she asked anyway. "What?"

"How are you feeling?"

"That's not what you're thinking."

"Lin."

"Come on. Just say it." She hated that she was about to lose to him.

"First the brick, now this attack on your truck."

"Someone doesn't want me around." She looked straight at him. His eyes oozed sympathy. "But why? The only people I know here are Corrine and Adam, and you, of course. But I guess we can rule you out as the attacker after tonight."

"Thanks." His mouth twitched up into a glimmer of the first genuine smile she'd ever seen on his face. Maybe death-defying car chases invigorated him. Maybe he just enjoyed winning arguments.

She arched her brow and shot him a fake smile. "I almost forgot. I've met The Muffin Man and your bitchy girlfriend, Ashley. Maybe Ashley's jealous."

The nascent smile faded from his lips. His eyes narrowed. "Ashley Cooper is not my girlfriend."

"So say you. Maybe she has a reason to be jealous."

"She is *not* jealous." He slid around in his seat. "Let's go. We can talk more about this in the morning."

But there was nothing left to say. She'd face a thousand Kens before she put Corrine or Adam, or even Jesse, in harm's way again. Her future was a question mark, but short-term she'd go back to the Klein campaign and try to fend off the senator until she found another job.

They drove home under a clear sky. The moon, just a thin sliver in the east, seemed to follow them. They topped the rise. The McCormicks' house stood alone, empty and still in the shallow valley. No lights shown in the windows. Corrine and Adam were still out. Jesse turned into the driveway, and the Silverado's headlights illuminated the garage.

She gasped. Jesse punched the brakes, and the truck screeched to a halt.

"What the—" He trailed off.

Over the garage doors, someone had spray-painted the words, *Go Home*. The fresh paint glistened in the high beams, and dripped onto the gravel below.

Chapter Eleven

The Possum had come up to Lake Forest to discuss the case. Mitty found him in the throne room. His sharp, hungry face suited the Old Man's lair, its dusky Persian carpet and gothic furniture.

She adjusted the silk scarf she'd wrapped around her bald head. She couldn't bear to put on her wig. It itched. Hell, everything itched. When she complained, the doctor told her she was depressed. He seemed proud of himself when he said this to her, as if he'd just made an amazing discovery.

The Possum extended a hand, and she shook it. "How are you feeling, ma'am?"

"I'm doing fine, thank you." She waved him toward the circle of chairs. "Please, sit."

He hunkered down on the Old Man's "throne" as she and Murphy used to call the massive burgundy velvet chair favored by their father. Two snarling lions jumped at each other across the carved wood frame behind The Possum's head and the armrests were held up by growling mahogany hounds.

The Possum eyed her uncertainly. "Did you want to sit here?"

She lowered herself into a plump Victorian parlor chair. "Please sit. I want to hear what you've found."

He settled himself on the throne and stared down at the carpet's red curlicues. Her heart sank. The news wasn't good.

"I've checked every database I know, searched under her first name, her last name, her social security number. I tried tennis and baby and twin. But nothing. I even called in a few favors."

"She's probably married so her last name wouldn't be Basinger anymore."

He tilted his head up. His small dark eyes gleamed at her. "I tried marriage records going back thirty years. No Murphy Basinger, east or west of here. Or south."

"I see." She hesitated. Should she ask? If she surrendered this little nugget, and it turned out to be fool's gold, how would she get through tomorrow or the next day or the next? She sighed. What difference did it make? Either she would live or she wouldn't. "Did you try Denver?"

The Possum's face registered surprise. He straightened. "Denver? Why Denver?"

Mitty slid her hand into the pocket of her cardigan and pulled out the page she'd torn from a glossy magazine in the hospital's waiting room. She handed it over.

"What is this?" he asked, staring blankly down at the page.

"It's an article about a senator from Colorado."

"Do you suspect your sister married him?"

"No." She pointed to the photo of Senator Klein surrounded by his staff. "See the girl standing next to the senator?"

The Possum frowned. "She doesn't resemble the picture you gave me."

True. But she did resemble Murphy's lover. Mitty had stared for hours at the picture of the grave girl, studying the shape of her face, trying to discern the color of her eyes from the grainy image, comparing the curve of her lips with the boy she barely remembered. Sometimes she was positive the girl was Murphy's daughter, other times she grew angry at herself for being delusional. "She looks like the father."

The Possum's eyes glittered with concern. "Ma'am, I know you are not well, but this would be a wild goose chase at best. I mean, what are the chances you would open up a magazine and find your long lost niece staring back at you?"

She snatched the page from his hands. "I am not paying you to analyze me, Mr. Petros. I am paying you to find my sister and her children." She stood up. "Find out who that girl is."

"Can I keep the photo?"

Her fingers squeezed the page until it crackled. "No. There are only ten people in the photo, and only one with blond hair.

You should be able to figure out which one she is once you fly to Denver, which I assume you'll do immediately."

His head nodded energetically.

"That's all." She stood up and waited for him to show himself out.

Chapter Twelve

"Did someone enter the Publishers Clearinghouse Sweepstakes?" Adam called out from the bottom of the driveway where he had been trying to repair the Silverado's cratered back bumper with a hammer and a can of silver paint.

Holding a greasy monkey wrench, Linnea stood next to Jesse, who was poking around under the Silverado's hood. She followed Adam's gaze. A black limo slithered down the rise.

Jesse looked up. "What is going on now?"

He sounded cranky and looked crankier. His faded flannel shirt hung askew on his broad shoulders, and his mud-caked work boots yawned wide. His skin was pale beneath his dark beard stubble, and the circles under his eyes matched the color of his hair. But he'd gone out again last night even though Teddy had discovered the pickup trailing them on Saturday night was a "stolen" Cooper Construction vehicle. Linnea tried not to feel betrayed, especially since Jesse had promised to check a funny noise under the Silverado's hood before she left for Denver—not drink beer and hang out with Ashley *frigging* Cooper.

"It's Ken," said Linnea. Behind her, the front door creaked open, and she knew that Corrine had come out on the porch.

"Ken? As in Klein?" asked Jesse.

"Yeah."

A fine tremor shook her fingers as she laid the monkey wrench on the gravel. She stuffed her hands in her jeans and stepped around the truck and past Adam to greet the limo. Ken's car halted at the foot of the driveway. The opaque windows seemed to stare at her, and she knew Ken was sitting in the back seat, watching.

Ken's driver got out first. Gary gazed at her in silent reproach over the roof of the limo. Then the front passenger door flung open, and a burly man in a leather jacket, dress slacks, and loafers squeezed out of the car.

He straightened up and examined Linnea closely. "The senator wants to speak to you."

Jesse's footsteps approached and stopped behind her. "I didn't realize you were key to the senator's organization."

"I should go see what he wants." But her feet refused to move.

The burly man breathed a pained sigh. Then he opened the back door, and Ken stepped out into the morning sunshine looking like a GQ model in his black silk suit and patent leather shoes that glittered under the bright Colorado sky.

He blinked a few times as his eyes adjusted to the daylight. His gaze flicked on each of the McCormicks. He smiled. "Nice to see you folks." His arms spread wide. "I hope my modest contribution helps you achieve your dreams for the future."

Ken chuckled as he took a few steps forward. His leather-soled shoes slipped on the shifting gravel, and he nearly tipped over. The burly man made a move to help him, but Ken stayed him with a flick of his wrist. He passed Linnea without looking at her and approached Jesse. He extended his hand. "Hello. Senator Ken Klein. I guess I'm at a bit of a disadvantage." He chuckled again. "You obviously know who I am, but I haven't met you."

Jesse rubbed his grease-streaked palms on his jeans before shaking the extended hand. "Jesse McCormick. Welcome to Cloud River, sir."

The turquoise house caught Ken's attention. His gaze skimmed over the garage, but he didn't seem to notice the fresh paint. He shook his head back and forth slowly as he surveyed the bright house, apparently overcome. "This is what Colorado is all about. Independent spirits creating a new tomorrow."

He turned back to Jesse. "Is this your place?"

"It belongs to my mother, sir."

"Call me Ken. Please. I feel like we're friends. You've been kind enough to house and feed my PR assistant for the past week or so." He forced a light laugh. "When she sets out to lend a helping hand, she pulls out all the stops."

"She had some trouble with her truck."

"Of course." Ken's condescending tone made it clear he didn't believe it.

Ken turned away from Jesse and surveyed the house again. "Impressive."

"Thank you, sir." Jesse held his body stiff and straight, like a soldier on parade, but his eyes studied Ken closely.

Ken noticed Corrine. She stood on the porch steps in her green caftan clutching a brown paper bag filled with bean sprout and cream cheese sandwiches, oatmeal cookies, and packets of herbal tea she packed for Linnea's departure. Ken advanced on her, slip-sliding on the gravel while managing to convey energy and high spirits. Although Linnea couldn't see his face, she knew he wore his get-out-the-vote expression: eyes crinkled at the corners and mouth smiling widely as if he were sharing a private moment with a lucky constituent.

He stopped at the bottom of the porch steps. "How do you do, ma'am?"

She smiled warmly. "Corrine McCormick, Senator. Welcome to our home."

"Corrine." He set one of his bright shoes on the lowest step and leaned his arms on his knee in a pantomime of folksy humility. "A lovely name. And unique, just like its owner."

Corrine frowned and for the merest second her mouth tightened. Then her smile returned, brighter than before. "Thank you." She set the paper bag on the porch railing and descended the stairs. "You must meet my youngest son, Adam. He was the one who wrote to your foundation."

Ken straightened up. "Absolutely. Nothing would give me more pleasure. Then, regrettably, we must go."

Adam nodded at Ken. "I'd shake your hand, but I don't want to get paint all over you."

"No problem, son." Ken patted Adam's shoulder manfully. "Thank you for all you've done for our country."

His eyes swung toward Linnea and locked on hers. "I thought we could ride back to Denver together."

"I have my truck here."

Ken nodded at the burly man. "I brought a driver along to bring it back."

Two hours in the back of the limo with Ken? Not a chance. Once Gary closed the divider, she'd be at Ken's mercy. "I'd prefer to drive back myself." She looked down at her old gray hoodie and salt-stained boots. "Besides I need to stop at the apartment to change."

"Nonsense."

Ken trekked up to her, and the sound of gravel shifting beneath his feet echoed in the thick silence. A light film of perspiration covered his face. The smell of sweat and aftershave rose from his skin. He pressed his hand to her waist.

"We can relax on the drive down to Denver. Catch up. I have some ideas I want to run by you for the campaign. Gary can drop you off at the apartment later."

His daily workouts kept him trim, but they also gave him strength. When she resisted the pressure of his hand, he curled his arm around her and propelled her forward effortlessly.

With a sinking heart, she surrendered.

"She said she wanted to drive herself back to Denver, sir." It was Jesse.

Linnea's feet froze. So did Ken's. Behind her back, the sound of Adam's uneven footsteps crunched against the gravel, then stopped near Jesse. The burly man lifted himself off the limo.

Even if Jesse and Adam outmatched Ken's bodyguard—a big "if"—attacking the security detail of a U.S. Senator could get them both tossed in jail for a long time. Linnea pulled away from Ken. Jesse and Adam stood shoulder to shoulder, hands curled into fists, legs planted wide, prepared to fight for her. She forced a stiff smile to her lips.

"I want to ride back with Ken." A frown crease Jesse's forehead. "Honest, Jess."

The whirr of an approaching car made everyone turn toward the road.

"Harry's here!" Corrine flung herself across the lawn. "He said he was going to come and say good-bye, Linnea. He wanted to surprise you."

A gray-green Prius appeared on the rise and honked brightly. When it pulled up behind the limo, Harry emerged with two pale blue bakery boxes. His eyes followed Corrine as she flitted toward him, her gown waving in the wind like the wings of a butterfly.

"We're so glad you came," Corrine said. She hugged Harry as tightly as the two boxes would allow and whispered in his ear.

Harry's expression sobered. His gaze swept the group, starting with Gary and traveling up the driveway past Linnea and Ken to stop at Jesse and Adam.

Corrine pressed a hand to his shoulder. "Come and meet our special guest."

"I'd be honored. Hope everyone likes muffins."

"Harry, this is the great Senator Klein."

Balancing the muffin boxes in one arm, Harry shook hands with Ken. "You are doing a fantastic job, Senator. You'll have my vote come November. I just want you to know."

"I appreciate your support, Harry." Ken's eyes slid to Linnea. "It's been a pleasure to meet you all—"

"Oh, Senator, wait." Corrine fluttered closer to him and slipped her arm through his. "You must stay a little longer and try one of Harry's famous muffins. In this corner of the state, he's the official Muffin Man."

"Great idea, Corrine." Harry turned to Ken. "If you're as thrilled with them as my customers, could you pass my name onto your caterer?"

Ken's eyes narrowed. "I don't—"

"No arguments, Senator. I couldn't live with myself if I let you go all the way back to Denver without a mug of ginseng tea and one of Harry's muffins. You look like a bran man to me," said Corrine.

She snuggled closer to him and leaned toward the house until Ken had to go with her or push her away. He gave in. Corrine dragged him up the drive.

"Thank heavens I cleaned yesterday, Senator," said Corrine. Her eyes slid sideways for a split second and caught Harry's. She nodded at the limo, before continuing her one-sided dialog with Ken. "If you thought the outside of our house is unusual, you'll really be amazed at the inside. I have ..." Her voice faded away as she pulled the politician up the front steps and into the house.

Harry winked at Gary and the bodyguard. "Better hurry, boys, before Senator Klein eats all the muffins." When neither man moved, Harry shrugged. "Suit yourselves. Of course, you probably heard that there's a mad man loose in this neighborhood slinging bricks into people's windows. Hit Linnea in the head the other night. Hope Corrine and the senator don't run into him."

The doors of the limo slammed simultaneously, and the two men slip-slided up the driveway, hands curled into fists, foreheads knitted into deep scowls. Harry followed them.

Jesse barked in Linnea's ear. "Greenhouse. Now." He strode around the side of the house and disappeared.

Adam winked at her. "Go on with Jesse. He can help you. I have a senator to entertain. Maybe he can stop the shopping center development."

In the doorway of the north greenhouse, Jesse stepped aside for Linnea, then closed and locked the door behind them. His long body slouched wearily against the wall, but his eyes flickered with irritation.

"What the hell happened out there?"

"What do you mean?"

"What do I mean?" He sounded incredulous. "I mean I almost got my ass kicked because you were afraid to get into the limo with our esteemed senator. I want to know why." He lifted himself off the door and began to pace.

She threw him a half-truth. "He wants to go out with me."

Jesse frowned at her "So? Just tell him 'no' if you don't want to."

"I did. He won't listen."

"Just keep saying 'no' until he gets tired of hearing it."

She dropped her gaze to her feet. "That isn't enough."

"Shit!" The word echoed against the glass-paned walls. He stepped closer to her. "Did he do something to you?" When she didn't move, he tried again. "I put myself on the line for you out there. So did Adam. We're on your side."

"It's complicated. If I drive myself back to Denver, I can manage the situation from there."

"Look at me." He pulled her to him. His voice was gentle, pleading. "Please Lin, look at me."

She raised her head and met his eyes. "I … It's nothing."

"Bullshit. Tell me the truth."

She let her shoulders slump. "A few days before I came to see Adam, we were in the limo, and … well, he just sort of reached over and grabbed me."

"Grabbed you?"

"Grabbed my breast and crushed it in his fist."

"Did he hurt you?"

She nodded. "I screeched and tried to push away from him, and he slapped me. Then he said we belonged together."

"What is it about politics and perverts?" His arms slid around her, and she dropped her forehead on his shoulder and pressed her palms into his back. "That's why you didn't want to get in the limo?"

"Yes." Pleasure snaked through her body as her waist brushed against his hips.

"Do you think Ken is behind the attacks here?"

"I can't imagine Ken, or Gary even, stealing a truck from the Cooper's construction yard and playing car chase." She shook her head regretfully. "It's not Ken's way. He's way too careful to do something that stupid." Jesse took a step back from her. "Can you file a harassment complaint?"

"I thought about it, but it's his word against mine. He'll say it was an accident, that the limo hit a bump or something. Gary will back him up. I'll look like a jealous woman out to destroy our handsome senator's career."

"Do you really want to go back to Denver? You'll be with him every day."

Her face began to burn. "I really want to stay here."

"Lin." He said her name softly. "I can barely feed Adam and Corrine."

"I know it's asking a lot, but it's just until I find a new job. I want to start over in Fort Collins or Greeley." *Or Cloud River?*

His Adam's apple bobbed beneath his dark stubble. "I guess you can stay until you find another job."

She threw her arms around his neck and hugged him. "When I'm not sending out my résumé, I'll be right here in the greenhouses helping you. I promise to work my fingers to the bone to keep those greedy bankers from taking Corrine's house away."

A startled expression flitted across his face, then the familiar boyish grin curved his lips. "Great."

"What is going on, Jesse? You aren't going to run off to Colombia?"

The grin faded from Jesse's lips, replaced by a hard, determined line. "No."

She put her hands on her hips and studied him closely. "Maybe I'm not the only story-teller around here."

"You have my word. I'm not going to Colombia."

Okay, maybe he wasn't going to Colombia, but *something* was up. "I don't bel—"

"Come here." He pulled her into his arms, cupped her jaw with his warm, rough hands, and pressed his mouth against hers. His lips were gentle as they caressed her mouth, his cheeks scratchy, his musky scent uniquely Jesse. The desire she'd felt before deepened into need. She slid her hands around his waist, leaned into him, and kissed him back until he drew away.

Emptiness throbbed inside her. "Please Jess." She lifted her arms and circled his warm neck, opening herself to him, and brushed his mouth with a feathery kiss.

His breath quickened, and his hands pressed against the small of her back, pulling her firmly against his hips. His eyes darkened with desire. "Am I hurting you?"

"No." Her body was on fire. It had been a long time since a man had kissed her. He closed his eyes and covered her mouth with a demanding kiss that swelled her need into hunger for his touch, his body, his complete possession. Her lips parted, allowing his tongue to trace the curve of her lips and slid across her teeth before exploring her mouth.

Her hands brushed the crisp hair at the nape of his neck and traced the curve of his hunky shoulders. He tasted of toothpaste and coffee and man. Her hips, held firmly against his, felt him harden. Her body quickened with desire, and she tightened her arms around his neck to pull herself closer to him.

"Linnea? Jesse? Where are you? The senator refuses to leave until he sees Linnea." It was Adam.

Jesse released her and pulled away. For a few moments he studied her, a slight frown creasing his forehead, then he glanced over his shoulder. "We better inform the senator that you'll be staying on for awhile."

Her face burned from the scrap of Jesse's beard. She patted her cheeks. "Do I look okay?"

"You look like you've just been kissed. Maybe you should wait here. I'll tell him you're working for me now."

As the greenhouse door banged shut behind him, her head cleared. He *was* hiding something. The kiss felt real, but it had also been an attempt to distract her. Angry voices rose from the front of the house. She raced to the sink to splash cold water on her face before joining the skirmish.

Ken and his entourage were crunching down the driveway. Jesse, Adam, Corrine, and Harry watched from the porch. Face flushed, eyes narrow slits in his aristocratic face, Ken was consumed with fury. When Linnea appeared, he stopped. His icy blue eyes raked her body.

"It's considered good business etiquette to give notice at your current job before you accept another." He pursed his lips. "You signed an agreement to write an article for the *Denver Post* about the McCormick family's misfortunes and how we tried to prevent their obvious decline." He sneered the last two words. "I expect you to honor it. Make sure it has plenty of pathos as we discussed."

He glanced up at the porch, then at Linnea again. His eyes gleamed with triumph. "What was that PR phrase you used? Oh yes. A three-hankie story."

He nodded to the McCormicks. "Good day, folks."

He walked off with as much senatorial dignity as the gravel driveway allowed and slithered into his limo.

Chapter Thirteen

The hurt creasing the corners of Corrine's eyes cut deep into Linnea. "Were you really going to write about us? Humiliate the family in front of the entire state of Colorado?"

"No, of course not."

"Was he making it up?"

"No. I mean, yes." *Oh, hell.* "When I first came, yes, that was the assignment. But—"

"How could you betray us? I took you into my home and treated you like my own daughter."

"Corrine, I swear I wouldn't have—"

The older woman flew into the house.

The men stared down at her. Jesse's expression was thunderous, and Adam's jaw gapped in surprise. Harry's forehead wrinkled with confusion. Linnea ran for the Silverado.

"Lin! Wait!"

Jesse's boots clattered down the porch steps as she slammed the truck door and turned the key in the ignition. The engine didn't turn over. "Dammit!" She tried again, jerking the key frantically. Nothing.

Through a film of tears, she watched Jesse's head appear at her window.

"What did you do to my truck?"

"Roll down the window."

She shook her head.

"I want to talk to you."

She stared straight ahead. "Just fix the truck so I can go."

"Not until you talk to me."

She rubbed her eyes and swiped at her nose. Then she pressed the button to lower the window. Nothing happened. She rolled her eyes. Would anything ever go her way?

The door swung open, and Jesse lifted her out of the Silverado and set her down in front of him. "I was checking the spark plugs when the senator arrived."

She turned away from him and stared at the rise in the road and the disappearing limo. "Just attach them so I can go."

"You're staying with us. Remember?"

"I can't. You all hate me."

"No one hates you."

"Well, you're mad at me."

"I'm not mad at you."

"Then why are you glowering?"

"I'm mad at our esteemed senator for acting like an asshole. Think about it. How can you write an article about how the veterans' fund helped us when I tore up the check?"

At least Jesse didn't hate her. "Actually, you shoved it at me."

He bent his head and looked at his feet. "Yeah, I guess I did. Sorry."

Her depression returned. "Corrine is really upset."

Jesse brushed a strand of hair out of her face. "Why don't you go back to the greenhouse and start packing up the lettuce? I'll talk to the others. When you're ready, you can explain things to Corrine."

What other choice did she have? Plan B was to leave Cloud River and return to Denver. "I guess you're right."

The gold sparks in his eyes danced. "Music to my ears."

*

Through the glass roof, the moon's pale light seemed far away. Linnea felt rudderless and alone. The greenhouse door squeaked on its un-oiled hinges, and Jesse stepped in, freshly showered and wearing a clean shirt. She hadn't expected red roses and declarations of love over one hot kiss, but she hadn't expected him fall back into Ashley's arms either. She sighed. At least he was honest. "Going out for a beer tonight?"

"Not exactly." He closed the door and came to her. "I haven't been truthful about where I go at night."

"Really? I was convinced you were a closet alcoholic."

"Linnea—"

She raised a hand before he could say more. "I don't know what you and Ashley have going on, but you don't owe me any explanation. Forget what happened between us this morning. I have." The scent of soap and his musky aftershave wove itself around her head like incense. *She'd never forget.*

His eyes narrowed. "What makes you think I'm seeing Ashley?"

"How naive do you think I am?"

"Is that a rhetorical question?"

"Come on, Jesse, give me a little credit. Why else would you get showered and go out after working all day? There has to be a woman involved."

"Oh, there is. I guarantee it."

"And it's fine. I got a little emotional this morning. You comforted me. It's over and done with."

He arched one dark brow. "If you say so."

Propping a hip against the trestle table, he studied her. "Corrine is in the kitchen finishing the dinner dishes. Now is a good time to go talk to her. I'm leaving, and Adam's at work. You'll have the house to yourselves. Besides, I don't want you in here at night unless I'm around."

She gazed at the light burning from the kitchen. The shadow of Corrine's head passed by the window, and a twinge of regret tugged at her. The longer she waited, the harder it was going to be to defend herself.

"Come on." Jesse pressed a warm hand to the small of her back. She set down her trowel and let him steer her outside. He switched off the lights in the greenhouse and locked the door before abandoning her on the back stoop.

Fingers of light from the kitchen poked through the dark house. She took baby steps forward, nervousness tugging at her like a persistent child. If Corrine wouldn't listen to her, she'd leave no matter what Jesse said. Her heart was thumping by time she reached the kitchen door. Corrine was filling the chipped enamel tea kettle at the sink. Linnea cleared her throat.

Corrine didn't look up. "Tell me the truth. Did you pick Adam's letter so you could feel better?"

Linnea's heart popped into her throat. Had Corrine guessed the truth about Marco and Adam? "I don't know what you're talking about."

"Your husband is dead, but I still have my son. Did you think you'd feel better if you could humiliate us? Make the whole state of Colorado sorry for the pathetic McCormicks who can't pay their bills?"

"Of course not." Linnea hated herself for feeling relieved.

"Then why did you pick him?"

She glossed over the truth. "I couldn't do anything for my husband, but I could still help his friend."

"You should have done your homework. The senator is right, you know. We're just dirt poor nobodies who aren't worth saving." Her face melted into despair. She gestured at the well-worn kitchen. "Robbie and I dreamed of building a simple, happy life for ourselves and our children. Now he's gone, and I'm going to lose everything we cared about. Our house and our land and my tea garden ..." A sob escaped her.

Her self-pity poked a raw wound inside Linnea. "How can you talk like that? You have everything in the world I've ever dreamed of."

"Like what?"

"Like a real family with sons who love you and would do anything in the world for you and a town full of friends like Harry. You won't lose those things if the bank forecloses on your house. You'll never be alone, Corrine."

Corrine slumped against the stove and buried her face in her hands. Her words were muffled, her tone soft and weary. "I am the most ungrateful human being in the world."

"No. You're my friend. I love you, too."

A shrill whistle made Corrine jump. She straightened as steam exploded out of the kettle spout. Linnea took a tentative step into the kitchen. "I'll get the cups out."

"I'll steep the tea."

Linnea pulled two earthenware mugs out of the cabinet, while Corrine scooped dried mint into the tea press. When the tea was brewed, she sat beside Corrine at the scratched kitchen table and stirred raw sugar cubes into her steaming mug.

"What will you do if you have to leave?" Linnea asked.

Corrine set her mug on the table. "I don't know. But I'll tell you what I won't do."

"What's that?"

"I won't sell this house to the Coopers so they can destroy it and build their obscene McMansions on my family's land. I'll find someone who wants to follow in our footsteps. Someone who will respect the earth and take care of the house and everything in it."

"Can you find someone like that?"

"Sometimes you just have to believe that good will triumph over greed."

"I do." Linnea hesitated. "Although my faith is a little shaky of late."

From the pocket of her hoodie, Supertramp began to blare. She pulled out her cell phone and glanced at the screen. "It's Ken."

Corrine stood up. "I have some clothes in the dryer. I better check on them." She whisked herself out of the kitchen, her thick-soled sandals clacking against the wood floor as she retreated.

Linnea pressed the phone to her ear. "Hello?"

"Where are you?"

"In Cloud River."

"They looked ready to throw you out when I left."

"Yeah. Thanks."

He got to the point. "You are a silly young woman." Ken's voice was ice cold. "You mistook what happened in the limo, and consequently you are making a fool of yourself and everyone around you."

She felt a cold trickle of fear roll down her spine. "What do you mean?"

"First of all, my true intentions, which I will only discuss face to face at the appropriate time, are beyond whatever childish scenario you are imagining. Secondly, my ultimate goal is marriage."

She could barely breathe. "But we don't love each other."

"Love," he scoffed. "Save your love for that overgrown G.I. Joe you're screwing."

"His name is Jesse, and I am not—" She couldn't say the word. "I am not sleeping with him."

"Come on, Linnea. You two were up to something while that muffin kook and the tea lady cornered me in the house."

"Did you call for a reason or just to insult me and my friends?"

"I called to put the offer of marriage on the table. With my political instincts and your youth and common touch, we will be a power couple to match any in Washington."

She didn't want to be the youthful half of a power couple. She wanted to be the member of a loving family. Like the McCormicks. "I'll never marry you."

"You will. I predict your cozy little nest in Cloud River will blow up under you, and you will be running back to me before midsummer. Then we will have that long talk about our future together. Good night, Linnea." He hung up before she could tell him he was crazy.

"What did he want?" Corrine was leaning against the doorway.

Linnea tried to sound casual. "He wants me to come back to Denver."

"Jesse said he hurt you. Is that true?"

She nodded.

"Then you can't go back there." Corrine slid into her chair.

"Thanks." Linnea sipped her tea and relaxed, letting the warmth of the homey kitchen work its soothing magic on her tired body.

Corrine eyed her. "If I tell you something personal, will you promise not to get upset?"

"Of course."

"I've been harboring this sort of fantasy that Jesse would fall in love with you and want to marry you, and you'd stay on here, and he'd make a go of rebuilding the organics business."

Definitely a fantasy. "You should have seen him Saturday night during the car chase. He's never looked so alive, I guess. Jesse isn't cut out to be a farmer."

Corrine's mouth quirked up ruefully. "I guess I've known that since he was a boy." Her gaze dropped to her lap. "What about you and Jesse?"

"There's an attraction. I won't deny it. But he's seeing Ashley, and I'm not in a good place right now." She tried to smile. "Bad karma. It's my destiny."

Corrine reminded her of Jesse as she arched an eyebrow. "Maybe it's not bad karma. Maybe it's bad timing. Much more fixable."

It was bad karma, and she did not want to discuss it. "You know what? I've been having a fantasy that you fall in love with Harry and move in with him."

"Harry is very special, and he feels the same way about me." Corrine sighed. "But I could never use Harry to solve my problems."

"So much for fantasies."

Another sigh escaped from Corrine. "Yeah, so much for fantasies."

"Maybe if we put our heads together, we can come up with a new Plan B for saving the farm."

Corrine's dark eyes filled with sadness.

"That was dumb thing to say. Sorry."

Chapter Fourteen

Creak! The hall floor moaned. Someone was creeping toward Corrine's bedroom door.

Linnea cracked open one eye and peered through the darkness. The bedroom wall and the nightstand loomed. Behind her, Corrine's regular breaths sawed through the dead-of-night silence. Linnea forced her lungs to match the same pattern then pretended to roll over in her sleep so she could see the door.

A large male shadow peeled away from the inky darkness framed inside the doorway and inched its way around Corrine's side of the bed. Linnea tried to quiet her spasmy lungs as he crept closer. He stopped behind her. She lay still, not daring to move a muscle, tensing as she waited for him to grab her or hit her. But he did neither. Instead he receded slightly, his movements slow and deliberate. There was a light rustle as he sifted through her clothes, the muted jingle of her keys as he moved her purse. If only she could see what he was doing.

The intruder took a deep breath, a sound she'd recognize anywhere. *Jesse!*

She pretended to sleep, absorbing the shock of this secret foray. He moved away from her. Through her half-closed eyes he was barely distinguishable from the dark walls as he slipped back into the hall and was swallowed by the night.

When the silence grew deep again, she sat up and took inventory. Her cell still rested on the nightstand beside Robbie's old clock radio. The glowing digits on the radio read four thirty. Her clothes lay in a heap beside the bed where she threw them last night. Why was he sneaking into her bedroom?

She surveyed the room one more time and yawned. Everything was just as it should be. She yawned again. She'd weasel the truth out of him tomorrow. She sank slowly against the pillows, pulled the blankets up to her chin and closed her eyes. Then her eyes popped open. She rolled over slowly so she wouldn't wake Corrine and peered through the dark at her heap of clothes again. Her shoulder bag was gone.

On the other side of the house, keys tinkled and the front door clicked open. Where was Jesse going? It was too late for him to visit Ashley, and way too early to start work in the greenhouse. Whatever he was planning, it was something he didn't want her or his mother to know about or he wouldn't be sneaking out of the house before morning. And why the hell did he need her purse?

Linnea grabbed her jeans from the bedroom floor and shimmied into them. She clutched the hem of her nightgown and swept it over her head, then pulled on her sweatshirt while her bare feet probed the floor for her boots and jammed into them. She swung out of the bedroom and tip-toed down the hall into the living room.

The front door cracked open and Jesse returned, muttering to himself. She flattened herself against the wall and prayed he wouldn't see her. Luck was on her side. He hurried past and disappeared into the kitchen.

*

"Idiot." He'd forgotten his papers.

Jesse stole back in the house to grab his backpack with the documents he'd need to give Keystone, plus all the spare keys he could scrounge up to the Honda and Silverado. He didn't want to discover a posse on his tail halfway to Winter Park.

He slung the backpack over his shoulder and tread back through the living room. Deep silence filled the house. This time he'd outfoxed the family. They'd be hurt and upset when he returned, but long-term, it was the only fix to their problems.

In the icy predawn, the van hummed softly at the curb. He'd parked it there last night so the crunch of gravel wouldn't alert the sleeping house. Slipping behind the wheel, he tapped the gas gently and rolled silently up the road. As the van cleared the rise, he flicked on the headlights and pressed the gas pedal to the floor. The van sailed toward the highway and Winter Park.

The miles separating him and Cloud River multiplied, and he began to hum softly to the radio. The weight of his worries drifted away like flotsam in a mountain stream, and his optimism returned. Two years was nothing. He was only thirty-one. He had plenty of time to build a good life—he just had to keep his head down and get the hell out of Nigeria in one piece.

Twenty miles out of Denver he watched dawn seep in from the east, its light sponged by a blanket of thick clouds spreading from the high plains into the Rockies. He pushed the van a little harder. If he beat the morning traffic around Denver, there'd be time to grab some breakfast before heading into the mountains. The van merged west onto I-70, and a lone snowflake flew toward him, melting against his windshield.

"Shit!" He hit the heel of his hand on the steering wheel and welcomed the faint ache against his wrist. What had he expected? Another flake drifted toward the van and splatted on his windshield. His foot pressed hard against the gas. If a storm hit, he had to be at the Keystone lodge before the roads closed.

After a few more flakes, the snow dried up. He took a deep breath and pushed on. West of the city, he pulled off the interstate to fill the van and grab some breakfast. As he jammed the pump into the van, Jesse stared uneasily at the sky to the west. It hung over the peaks, bruised and ominous. He hurried into the mini-mart.

A grizzled woman in an over-sized lumberjack shirt stood behind the counter. "Looks like snow, don't it?"

Jesse stirred powdered creamer into his acrid coffee. "Yeah. Just hope it holds off for a few more hours. I have an appointment near Winter Park."

"Don't seem like it's gonna." The woman glanced through the store window while Jesse plunked the coffee and a wilted breakfast sandwich on the counter and dug in his back pocket for his wallet.

The old woman frowned at him. "Nothin' for the gal?"

"Gal?"

She held up a hand. "Forget it. Just thought I'd ask."

Jesse's heart began to race. "You saw a girl out there?" He glanced through the window. The van sat alone among the pumps.

The woman slid a finger under the black wool stocking cap pulled over her wiry gray hair and scratched. "A blond gal with those furry boots they all like to wear these days."

Did he miss a set of keys? Had Lin followed him here? *Impossible.* If she tailed him out of Cloud River he'd have spotted her, wouldn't he? But his eyes turned to the window, searching the street for the Silverado.

Behind him, the old woman said, "Probably went to the washroom. That's where she was headed."

He flung three twenties on the counter. "I'll be right back for my change."

Jesse poked his head around the corner before creeping towards the door inset into the enameled white brick. When Lin came out, he'd grab her before she could make a run for the Silverado.

The washroom door squeaked open, and Lin emerged, nearly colliding with him. He grabbed her arm.

"What the hell are you're doing here?"

She screeched. Her free hand pressed hard against his chest. When she saw it was him, her resistance ebbed. She pulled at her arm. "Let me go."

"Not until you tell me what you're doing here."

A nest of snarls hung in the back of her hair. Her lips were pale and cracked. She wore a thin hoodie, useless against the frigid morning air. But her chin rose, and although he was taller, she managed to look down her nose at him. "Me? What are you doing here?"

He had nothing to hide. "I'm doing what's necessary to help my family."

Her eyes swept the length of him scornfully. "If you're so sure of yourself, why are you sneaking out in the middle of the night? And why did you steal my purse?"

"I did not steal your purse."

"You did."

"I confiscated your keys so you'd stay put until I got back."

"Because you know you're wrong." She twisted her wrist to loosen his grip, but he held tight.

"Where'd you hide the Silverado?"

She looked blank. "The Silverado?"

A sinking feeling spread across the pit of his stomach. "Did you stow away in the van?"

"You didn't give me any choice." She had the nerve to roll her eyes at him. "After you snuck out of my room with my purse—"

"How you folks doing? You okay, young lady?" The cashier eyed them from the corner of the mini-mart.

He released Lin's arm. "Don't you dare start a scene," he whispered through gritted teeth.

Lin managed a gracious smile. "I'm fine. We're just discussing our route for today."

The woman's eyes narrowed. "You sure?"

"Positive. See?" Lin slid an arm around his waist and nestled against him. Her cheek brushed his chin. His loins tightened, and he struggled to keep his hand from touching her skin.

The woman nodded. "Got your change ready inside," she said to Jesse.

"We'll be right in."

She nodded again and disappeared.

Lin retrieved her arm and faced him. Her big gray eyes pleaded with him. "Look, Jess. I can't make you turn around—"

"You mean you're not going to cry rape and get me locked up?

You and Corrine would know just where to find me for the next twenty years."

Her eyes narrowed. Fine-boned, fisted hands rested on her hips. "Maybe I'm not as *accommodating* as your girlfriend, but at least I care about you."

"She is not—" He stopped. Ashley's imaginary roll as his girlfriend was keeping Lin at a safe emotional distance. After the kiss they'd shared, that's where he wanted her. Far, far away. One abyss at a time. "Forget it."

Lin frowned. "Whatever." She came at him again. "Just listen to me. If you're giving up two years to help Corrine, why not do it on the farm? Your father made it work. Why can't you?"

She was the most stubborn woman he'd ever met. "Don't you think I've thought about that? For your information, I love my mother and my brother. I don't want to hurt them. But if you—they—would stop being emotional about this, you'd realize it won't work."

Her voice grew louder and higher. "Why, Jesse? Give me one reason why." The bitter wind had burned her cheeks red. Her arms were wrapped tightly around her body to hold in the warmth. He wanted to pull her against him, shield her from the gusts coming off the mountain, and press her soft body against his. But he didn't.

"Robbie worked that farm for thirty years, and he struggled to make ends meet even after his best harvests. He was always behind. Most years he had to borrow from the bank just to buy seed. He kept at it out of love, but it's not a viable business. What happens after two years? I'm stuck. Either I stay on to meet expenses and pay the note or I leave and we're right back where we started."

"There's lots of regular jobs in Denver that pay well."

He shook his head. "None that will pay me a salary and signing bonus like Keystone. Besides, my resume doesn't exactly say corporate." He gazed into her troubled eyes. "The house is gone either way, but if I can pay the back taxes and mortgage, at least

Corrine will be able to sell the house and bank the Cooper money. That's the best I can do."

She dropped her head. "What if something happens to you?"

He touched her shoulder. Her body shivered beneath his hand. "I'm sorry."

She nodded without looking up.

"Come on. Let's get you something hot to drink."

"Wait." Digging into the pocket of her jeans, Lin pulled out the keys to the van. "I didn't want you to take off without me."

Something inside him shifted. He suppressed a smile as he snatched the keys from her outstretched hand.

She let him lead her around the building, his treacherous hand resting lightly at the small of her back, just above the swell of her hips. "What happens now?"

"Unless you want to wait here, you're coming with me."

They rolled out of the gas station and joined the interstate. Lin sat beside him chewing thoughtfully on a donut, a cup of hot chocolate clutched between her thighs. They'd barely gone a mile when a snowflake sailed out of nowhere and hit the windshield. Lin twisted her head sideways and studied the sky.

"Looks like snow. I didn't see any chains when I was hiding in the back."

"The van has snow tires. Besides, I'm only going another fifty miles. We'll be back in the lower elevations before any warnings go up."

She relented. "Well, I've only seen a few flakes. Maybe the worst will miss us."

"Yeah."

But the flakes began to multiply until the road in front of them looked like an eiderdown factory. The highway took a sharp curve north, and a blast of wind rocked the van. The Subaru Forester in front of him momentarily disappeared into a swirl of white.

"Are you sure——"

He shook a finger at her. "Not a word. I have an appointment in Winter Park, and I am going to keep it. Are we clear?"

"Whatever." But her tone said she thought he was an idiot.

And maybe he was. As the van pushed its way up the steep grade into the Rockies, the snow began in earnest.

Chapter Fifteen

Jesse pushed the van as fast as he dared and made good time climbing the nearly vertical grade into the mountains. Considering the crappy conditions.

But when he veered off the interstate just west of Idaho Springs, the driving got dicey. The wind had nearly erased the only road into Winter Park. The faint ridges of snow left by the plows and a thick forest of Douglas fir on either side of the highway were his only guide. He navigated along the serpentine road with growing unease. Not a single vehicle passed them. If the van slid off the road, it could be days before help came.

He glanced over at Lin. Her face was pale.

"Are you okay?"

She nodded. "Fine. I'll be better when we get there."

"Yeah. Should be just a few more miles." He turned back to the road. They passed under a tall Douglas fir. Its top branches, heavy with snow, bent precariously toward the road. As they drew near, a loud crack shattered the air. Jesse pulled the wheel hard to the left, skirting the range of the tree, and the van fish-tailed across the road. He steered into the skid and held his breath. The van righted itself inches from a snow bank. He began to breathe again.

Lin gasped and twisted around in her seat. His eyes shifted to the rearview mirror. Behind the van, a six-foot section of the tree crashed into the road.

She turned to him, wide-eyed. "I hope your friend has extra beds."

He hoped so, too.

He pressed lightly on the accelerator. The van's tires spun beneath them. "Come on, baby," he whispered under his breath. He put the van into reverse and rocked back, then pushed it into first gear and depressed the gas pedal again. "Come on. Just a few more miles." The van groaned, and after a loud, clanking protest, it lurched forward again.

Lin sighed in relief.

"Keystone's lodge should be coming up soon. It's before the town. Look for a sign on the right side of the road. I'll take the left."

Lin turned her head as he gently eased into second gear, and the van valiantly huffed and chugged its way up to Winter Park.

"There! I see it." Lin bobbed up and down in her seat.

He squinted at the snow-spattered sign up ahead. Through the thick flakes blowing across the windshield, *eyston odg* appeared. A surge of relief shot through him. Tapping gently on the brakes, he slowed the van to a crawl and turned in between the sign and a wrought iron lamp. The globe was dark and snow-covered. He felt a twinge of doubt. In a heavy storm, with visitors expected, Keystone should have it on.

Snow drifts were piled high on the driveway. It didn't appear that any vehicles had passed this way since the storm began. The underbelly of the van wasn't clearing the snow, and the front fender pushed the snow forward for several feet then stopped as the wall of snow grew too high to plow forward. Jesse put the van in park.

"This is a far as we go, I guess."

Lin didn't look at him. "Seems that way."

He peered out the windshield at the thick curtain of snow. "I can't see the lodge."

"How far is it from the road?"

"Don't know."

"Can you call and tell him you're here? Ask him to send someone down to help us."

He pulled his cell out of his jacket and pressed Keystone's number. The phone rang eight times before going into voicemail. "It's Jesse McCormick. I'm at the lodge. Call me."

He slid the phone into his pocket and stared out at the storm. "Let's hope he calls sooner rather than later." He met Lin's eyes. She looked frightened. "It's okay," he said softly. Anger at himself for putting her in danger surged through him. He pulled out the phone and dialed again. This time Keystone picked up.

"Glenn?"

"McCormick. I heard it was really storming up there."

"Where are you?"

"We rerouted to Cabo. Couldn't land in the storm."

"What about Nigeria?"

"Look, man, I'm sorry. It's not going to work out. My injured pilot came back early." Was this payback for standing Keystone up?

A gust of wind rocked the van and the falling snow spun like a dervish. "Look, I'm sort of stuck in your driveway. I may have to bunk here tonight."

"Sure. No problem. There's a key under the blue pot furthest from the door."

"Thanks." For nothing.

Children screamed in the background. "Look, man, I've got to ring off." The phone went dead.

Jesse dropped his head and closed his eyes and tried to remember the prayer his Baptist roommate taught him in college. But it refused to come to him. Instead, Robbie's voice, quoting the Tao, pushed through his despair. *To know you have enough is to be rich.* He wanted to break something.

A light hand slid over his shoulder and rubbed his back. "Are you okay?"

For Lin's sake, he pulled himself together and raised his head. He couldn't look at her. "The storm diverted his plane so he's in Mexico."

"What about the job?"

"There is no job." The words tasted sour in his mouth. Outside the van, the storm was rapidly turning into a full-blown blizzard.

"We'll have to wait out the snow. Stay in the van. I'll go see how far the lodge is from here. Maybe I can scrounge up a jacket for you."

"No way. I'm going, too."

He forced himself to face her. Her round eyes studied him. "You don't have a coat. Besides, what if I get lost in the storm?"

She patted his arm and half-smiled. "If you get lost in the storm, we'll both freeze to death. Me in here, you out there. Personally, I'd prefer dying with someone to talk to."

He grinned despite himself, grateful she was with him. "Great. The last words I ever hear will be yours, telling me to cheer up, everything will look better tomorrow."

"It will." She unbuckled her seatbelt. "Where is that old army blanket I hid under? It will have to be my coat."

The fierce north wind blew into his face. Hunched over, he walked blindly forward with Lin at his side. His feet and hands throbbed, and his legs ached. Ice crystals clung to the stubble of his beard and melted snow dripped into his eyes.

He glanced over at Lin, squinting to shield his eyes from the driving snow. She held the blanket tight at her throat, his man-size glove bunched around her small hand. Strands of hair stuck to her face and neck. He hooked his arm securely around her shoulder and pulled her close, trying to protect her from the wind. She looped her arm around him and held tight to his waist.

Lining the drive, a fence of split logs served as a ghostly trail marker. As he faced the fury of the howling arctic wind, it seemed easier to go with it than fight it, and twice he swerved off the drive and nearly smacked into the fence. Each time he righted himself, dragged his aching body and Lin to the approximate center of the driveway and pushed forward. But he lost precious time and body heat. Despair gripped him like a fist, and he glanced behind them. The blowing snow had already erased their footprints.

A brutal blast of wind nearly pushed Lin off her feet, and even he struggled to stay upright. He thought he heard her cry out.

"Come on, baby. We're almost there," he said, although the howling wind made it impossible for her to hear him. Maybe it was better that his words were blown away since it wasn't the truth. He didn't know where they were.

The drive curved into a stand of trees, bringing a small respite from the storm. He stopped and turned Lin toward him. Beneath the olive green blanket she peered up at him, the physical strain of battling the wind and snow etched on her face. He wanted to kiss away her pain. "Are you okay?"

She nodded, but her jaw seemed frozen and her lips were blue and quivering with cold. He pressed his mouth against hers. Then he slid an arm over her shoulder and pushed on.

A growing brightness ahead of them signaled a clearing. His pace picked up, and her arm squeezed his waist.

It took him a few minutes to find the front door. He had to kick at the snowdrifts against the house until his toe hit a step. But once he located the door and brushed at the snow until he uncovered the blue planter, they were quickly out of the storm and standing in a cold, ghostly gray great room.

Jesse flicked a nearby light switch. Nothing happened. "Power's out."

Pale light pressed against the wide windows on either side of the room. His eyes made out a short flight of steps descending into the center. An open fireplace of fieldstone rose up to the ceiling. Sofas piled high with cushions and low tables crafted from unfinished pine circled the fireplace. A neat stack of firewood waited for Keystone's next ski party.

He took Lin's hand. "Let's get the fire going."

Chapter Sixteen

The howling wind spun snow around the lodge in great white waves, making it impossible for Linnea to see if it fell from the sky or lifted up from the deep drifts hugging the mountainside. The thickening gloom was her only clue that above the heavy clouds, the sun was dipping into the west.

A night alone with Jesse edged closer. Her belly tightened with desire. Then she reminded herself that he was sleeping with Ashley. It was dangerous to want someone who didn't want you. Marco had taught her that lesson. Pulling herself together, she turned back to the fire and checked the skewered hot dogs warming in the flames.

"You look like a ski bunny." Jesse appeared from the kitchen with two goblets of wine.

She glanced down at the European-cut ski pants and the pale yellow cashmere sweater she wore. "My entire wardrobe doesn't cost as much as this outfit."

"Mine either." He'd dug out a pair of Flint-T cargo ski pants and a vintage Icelandic ski sweater in chocolate brown from Glenn Keystone's closet. In the fire's glow, his skin shimmered like gold against the dark sweater. Black stubble framed his wind-burned mouth. The planes of his face were sharp and strong. Only the strain around his eyes betrayed the frustration and worry gnawing at him.

"I found more gas in the shed," he said.

"How much?"

"Enough to keep the generator running for a few days."

A few days? She'd never make it. If they weren't rescued soon, she and Ashley Cooper were going to be sharing a lover. "I'm sure we'll be rescued before then."

"Maybe." Jesse's feet brushed against the steps as he descended into the party pit, and when she looked up again, he handed her a glass of the wine. Then he retreated to the sofa behind her and sank into the cushions.

She took a sip of the fruity wine. "Very nice. Thanks."

He studied her until she squirmed.

"What is it, Jesse?"

He took a quick gulp from his glass. "I tried to tell you this the day of the senator's visit, but you wouldn't listen. I have a second job. That's where I go at night. I haven't slept with Ashley since you came to town."

Why was he telling her this now? But she knew. He wanted to sleep with her so he was tearing down the barricades. Her cheeks burned, and she looked away. "I don't understand. How does she fit into your life?"

"I was at a low point when I came back to Cloud River, and Ashley was at loose ends." He paused. "She was my high school girlfriend. It just seemed to happen."

"You were at a low point because you had to quit the army?"

His expression grew bleak. "Sort of." Something Corrine said floated through her memory. *He lost the woman he loved because of me.*

She shouldn't ask, but she had to know. "Who was she?"

He straightened up and took a gulp of wine. "I just told you, Ashley is not my girlfriend."

His dishonesty hurt. "Don't play with me, Jesse."

His knuckles, wind-burnt and raw, tightened around the stem of the glass.

"Tell me. Please."

His gaze shifted to the fire, and the gold flecks in his eyes danced with the flames as he considered his response. "She was a general's daughter."

"Marriage?"

"We were talking about it." He grew silent again.

It was time to excuse herself and ransack the lodge for a chastity belt. She didn't do hook-ups, and he was still pining after his lost love. Plucking the skewers out of the flames, she laid the charred hot dogs on the platter resting by her feet. "I'll go scrounge up some plates. Maybe there's a can of beans in the pantry to go with this."

The ghost of a genuine smile hovered on his lips. "Don't go, Lin."

"Jesse, I don't—"

"Ask me anything."

A gust of wind shook the lodge and rattled the roof. A stream of white flakes blew by the window. Then the inky night settled in around the lodge. She could barely breathe. "What happened?"

"When I resigned my commission, she broke it off."

Linnea couldn't move. "Why?"

"She didn't approve of the disruption to our plans."

"What plans?"

"Conquer the world, of course. Have it all."

Disappointment rocketed through her. "Is that really your dream?"

"Isn't it yours?" A look of pure defiance crossed his face.

"I don't believe you. You're the guy who sacrificed everything for country and family."

"Grow up, Lin. I'm not noble, I'm a loser." He shook his head. "Don't you get sick of taking orders? Kowtowing to people like the senator? Never being able to give the ones you love the good things everyone else takes for granted?"

She sprang to her feet. "Good things? Like what? What 'good thing' requires you to sell yourself to the highest bidder? How much did you pay to have Corrine and Robbie for your mom and dad? What's the going price for a great brother like Adam?" She patted her chest. "Because I'll sell myself out any day of the week to buy those 'good things.' Just name the price."

The light in his eyes dimmed, and the defiance drained from his face. "It's been a really shitty day. I don't want to fight with you."

He leaned back against the cushions. His shoulders, always so strong, sagged. His hands, square and feathered with dark hair, rested on his knees, the long fingers pale against his black ski pants. She studied them. Would they be gentle against her skin, or impatient and demanding?

"What about me?" Her voice had stopped working so she whispered the question.

"I don't know." He stood up. "More wine?"

Her cheeks burned. "No."

When he disappeared into the kitchen, she rose. The little bedroom where she changed earlier was cold and dark, but right now it seemed like the safest place in the lodge.

"Where are you going?"

"My bedroom. I'm tired."

"Come sit with me." His voice was warm.

"I can't. It's not a good idea."

"Why not?"

"Come on, Jesse."

His glass clinked against the table as he set it down. "You're my friend, Lin. A true friend I can count on to stick with me when everything blows."

Anger burst inside her. "A *friend*? Why don't you just get a dog? Or call Teddy."

"You're being dramatic."

She put her hands on her hips and faced him. "So let's say that I agree to, ah, be your *true* friend. What do I get from you?"

He skirted the table and closed in on her. "I'm trying to be straight with you here. I want to be with you tonight, and I'm pretty sure you want to be with me. Isn't that enough?"

"No." She turned away.

He took a step closer. His breath was hot against her neck. "You've done so much to help my family. Don't you see? You're special. If you ever need me, I'll have your back. I promise."

"So I'm more than Ashley but less than the general's daughter."

His voice was tight. "There will never be a general's daughter again. It was a mistake."

"Just because your heart was broken doesn't mean you shouldn't try again."

"She didn't break my heart." His protest pushed through gritted teeth. "That's a ridiculously romantic notion with no basis in reality. I broke our mutual understanding by resigning my commission. She reacted logically."

Her heart did a little flip. She could almost hear his logical brain whirring out "reasonable" explanations for his break-up so he wouldn't have to accept that he hurt. She wanted to hold him, soothe him, make love to him. Anything to ease the pain etched on his face. She pressed her hand against his arm. "She was blind or stupid or both to let you go."

A log fell into the ashes. Jesse didn't move. His thick muscles twitched beneath her fingers. "I need someone I can trust." His hands gripped her shoulders. "I was hoping it would be you."

She swallowed. "I want you in my life."

"As a friend."

He was so close, she could count the corded ridges in his neck. It hurt to surrender—she wanted so much more from him—but he was in pain. He needed her. "As a true friend."

His face softened, and he smiled at her. "You won't regret this. I promise."

Not tonight, maybe, but eventually.

She let him gather her in close and pull out the elastic holding her ponytail. With a shake of her head, her hair fell around her like a veil.

"Put your arms around me, Lin." His lips were inches from her mouth. They brushed across hers until she raised her arms to his neck and pressed her body against the solid length of him. He was warm and smelled of wood smoke.

Tilting his head, he captured her mouth and pushed her lips apart. She greeted his first thrust with the tip of her tongue, sparring with his playfully. Jesse's breath grew harsh and quick, emboldening her. She bit his lips, then pulled them into her mouth and sucked.

His palms began a long, languid journey up her back, then down again. His touch was soft, gentle, as if he was memorizing the curve of her spine. His fingers traced her bottom and pressed her against his hips. He was hard.

"This is what you do to me, baby."

"Hmmm." That felt so good. She rubbed her hips against him until her body melted into hot liquid. "Do you like it when I do this?"

He growled in her ear.

She sank to the floor, dragging him with her.

Pulling her onto his lap, he buried his hands in her hair and dropped hungry kisses along her jaw. His lips found the lobe of her ear and suckled. Masculine breath rasped against her ear, bristly beard scraped against her cheek. Her legs fell apart.

"You taste so sweet." He breathed the words against the column of her neck, sending a shiver of pleasure through her. His fingertips traced her inner thighs, stopping short of her throbbing core.

"Jess." She trailed her palms down the front of his sweater, letting her hands curve over his hard muscles and ribs. Beneath her fingers, his broken heart pounded. She lifted his sweater and pressed her mouth against the fluttering skin and felt its strength. He would heal.

His erection pushed against her hip, demanding attention. She groped for his zipper, her mouth dropped from his chest to his waist.

A strong hand clutched her shoulder and pulled her away. She raised her eyes to his face and met a pair of glazed green eyes. "It's been awhile, huh?"

Her cheeks began to burn. He kissed them softly.

"Me too, baby, but let's slow it down. We got all night."

His lips touched the sensitive indent at the base of her neck. In a thick, husky voice, he whispered, "I like you hot and sexy." His mouth moved along her jaw to her other ear. "You reminded me of Alice in Wonderland the first time we met." He pushed the cashmere sweater off her shoulders, pinning her arms. He bent his head and traced the valley between her breasts with his tongue.

"And now?"

"I began to notice you were a woman our first day in the greenhouse." He dropped his head and watched his palms slide over her breasts. Her nipples beaded as he brushed over them.

Damn! He was driving her wild. She curled around his shoulders, wanting to melt into him, and buried her nose in his hair. Her lips brushed the top of his head. "I thought you were hot the second I saw you."

He squeezed her breasts gently. "I get that a lot."

"Really?"

He laughed. "No. Just making sure Alice is still somewhere inside the sexy woman on my lap."

He liked her. Tenderness squeezed at her heart. She went in for a deep kiss to hide the affection she felt for him. "You're bad."

"You don't know the half of it."

His fingers slipped beneath her sweater, brushing up her belly until they cupped her breasts over her thin cotton bra. His head tipped up. His eyes grew serious. "If I do anything you don't like, all you have to do is say 'stop.'"

She was his forever. "I know."

"Take off your sweater."

She gripped the hem of the sweater and pulled it up. Before she'd tugged it over her head, he'd unhooked her bra. She pushed her hair out of her eyes to find him gazing at her breasts. Self-conscious, she leaned into him.

His hands closed over her shoulders and tipped her back. "I knew they'd be beautiful."

She'd always felt ashamed of her breasts. "They're a little small."

"They're perfect." He drew circles around her nipples with his fingers, slowly tracing her curves, deliberately teasing her until her throat was making little groaning noises.

She pulled at his sweater. "I want to see you." And feel his skin against hers.

He kissed the top of each breast. "Don't go anywhere," he whispered to them. She felt them pebbled against his raspy voice.

He pulled off his sweater, exposing long, sinewy muscles sharply defined beneath his golden skin. A dark nest of hair covered his chest, tapering as it trailed down his body to his waist. She traced the dark line from his heart to the waistband of his pants where it disappeared. She rubbed his hard ridge and felt the heat of him. Now?

He pulled her hand away.

"I'm sorry. I didn't mean—" Men didn't like aggressive women. She'd learned that lesson well from her husband.

"Don't be."

"Then what do you want?"

"I want you with me every step of the way."

"I hope I remember how."

"Stop trying to manage. Feel. Isn't that what you always tell me?"

She closed her eyes and tried not to worry about satisfying him.

His fingers slid inside the back of her ski pants and played with the elastic of her panties before pushing in further to knead her bottom. Her thighs ached for him, her body was throbbing. Her head fell back, and he dipped his head and playfully circled one of her breasts with his tongue. She wanted him inside her. "I'm way ahead of you."

"Come back. Stay with me." His mouth, warm and velvety, closed over her breast, licking and sucking at the nipple. The heat of him burned through his pants branding her thigh. She twisted around and straddled him.

"Catch up with me."

He suckled on the tip of her other nipple until her knees tightened around his waist. Straightening up, he slid a hand into the pocket of his pants and pulled out a strip of condoms. "Compliments of Glenn. But I could only find five."

She bit one of his small brown nipples. Her need for him turned into an ache. "Then we better make this memorable."

A genuine smile lit his face. He lifted her off his lap and laid her down on the soft carpet in front of the fire. She began to pull at the zipper of her pants, but he laid his hand over hers and unzipped them himself. He pulled them off and grinned at her flowered cotton panties.

"I have some black ones back in Denver that are sort of silky."

"These are just the sort of panties I dreamed you'd wear."

She raised her arms and tussled his hair. "Have you been fantasizing about my underwear?"

He brushed a hand from her knee to the top of her thigh. "Maybe." When his fingertips touched the leg band of her panties, they slid underneath the elastic and brushed at the pale hair between her legs.

She arched into his hand, needing his touch on the center of her desire. He grinned wickedly as he lay down beside her. His fingers threaded through her hair and he kissed her, while her body screamed for release.

"Jesse."

"I got you, baby." He swung a leg between hers and pushed them apart. His hand trailed down her chest to her hips and slid inside her panties. His fingertips brushed over her. She gasped with pleasure and her legs fell apart.

Her hands pulled at his zipper.

He pushed her hand away again. A long finger slipped inside her, and he lifted his head and kissed her eyelids. "Close your eyes. Let me please you." The crease in his forehead had smoothed, and the tight knot of worry that weighed at the corners of his mouth was gone. He looked so handsome and young, her heart ached for him.

She closed her eyes. He drew her panties down her legs and over her ankles, then shifted before he unzipped his pants. His body settled over hers. His manhood burned her thighs, and she arched her hips. But he pulled back. Then his body ebbed downward. He pushed her legs wide apart and knelt between them.

"You are beautiful." The pad of his thumb rubbed her nub and her body coiled.

"Hurry. Or I'll come without you."

"You said memorable." His breath warmed her belly, then his head was between her legs.

He pushed her knees apart again. "Let me taste you." His fingers slid inside her. "You're so wet." Then his hands scooped up her bottom, raising her hips up, and his tongue explored the core of her, making its ways to her throbbing center, stroking lightly.

Her body pushed up to him, seeking release. Her desire tightened. "Oh, Jesse."

Abruptly, he drew away. A whimper of protest formed in her throat. There was the tear of the foil packet and his breath was sharp as he drew it on, then he was lying over her.

Her fingers combed through his hair and over his shoulders. His erection pressed against her, and this time when she raised her hips to him, he pushed into her. Slowly, gently. She groaned and dug her fingers into his back, urging him deeper. With a sharp intake of breath, he plunged into her, stretching her until she took him in, filling her.

"Ride me." He groaned the words into her ear.

Lifting her legs, she wrapped them around his waist and clung to his powerful, thrusting body. He pushed into her, burying himself deep inside her, his breathing harsh and irregular. Her coiled body shattered against him and pulsed, and she cried out. He stiffened in her arms, buried his face in her neck and drove hard into her again before he collapsed.

Her arms tightened around his sweat-dampened body. She sighed. "That was amazing."

He rolled away from her. "You were hot, baby."

Hot? Her after-glow dimmed. They were friends with benefits, and she'd be wise to remember it. "Yeah, you too," she said and turned on her side so he couldn't read the disappointment in her face.

Chapter Seventeen

Linnea opened her eyes. The dying logs in the fireplace glowed in the dark. Jesse lay beside her on the floor snoring softly. He stirred and flipped away from her, taking the blanket with him. Frigid air hit her backside and she shivered. Her hand pulled at the edge of the blanket. It didn't budge.

She scooted closer to him and slid her arms around his waist to soak in his body heat and studied the small tattoo on the back of his shoulder. A bow pulled taut by a ghostly hand, a silvery missile caught in its string. She kissed it.

"What are you doing?"

"Kissing your tattoo."

"Why?"

"I'm cold. You stole the blanket."

He raised his arm. "Pull."

She pulled at the blanket until her back was covered. "Why do you have a bow and missile on your back?" She kissed it again and snuggled closer to him.

"It's a longbow. I flew an Apache Longbow helicopter in Afghanistan," he said tightly.

"Don't you usually shoot an arrow from a longbow?"

He coughed. "It's a Hellfire missile. That's what Apache Longbows are armed with."

She rubbed her hand over it and pecked at the Hellfire missile with her lips. "I like it on your back. It's sexy." She pressed her nose close to his skin. He smelled musky and masculine.

"It's back there so Robbie and Corrine wouldn't see it and have heart failure. *Stop kissing me.*"

Hurt, she released him and scooted back. "Sorry. I didn't mean to bother you."

He flipped over. A thick erection pressed against the blanket. "You're not bothering me. You're driving me crazy." Her eyes flew up to his face. He rewarded her with one of his rare smiles. "It could be a few days before we're dug out. With four condoms left, we may have to get creative."

She propped her head in her hands and looked into his eyes. They glittered with desire. Her need for him made her ache. Her mouth found his lips, and she kissed him. "Hmmm. Can I go first?" She didn't wait for his answer. Her fingers pushed the blanket away and tightened around the erect soldier.

He threw his head back. "Lin, baby, no."

"Yes. You did me." She couldn't make him love her, but she could even the score. Maybe she'd feel like she was on firmer ground.

She bent her head and teased his swollen penis with her tongue. Her hands, trained in the backseat of an old Dodge Dart, touched and caressed all his secret places. Jesse's hips bucked. She took him in her mouth. His hand pressed against her shoulder and his hips pushed up until his body released. He groaned and sank back into the blankets. She kissed his belly, then lay down beside him again.

He turned and hugged her. "You didn't have to do that."

She rubbed her nose against his chest. "Sure I did. At least if I wanted you to walk again."

"True." He pulled her against him. His lips moved in her hair. "Do you miss your husband?"

She tried to sit up, but he held her tight against his body. "That's not exactly pillow talk."

"Seems like a fair question. You know your way around a man, and since you were a kid when you married and don't strike me as a cheating woman, I assume you learned how use that sweet mouth of yours from loving your husband."

She didn't want to discuss Marco. "It's complicated."

"Which means you don't want to talk about it."

"Yes."

"I won't judge you."

Wouldn't he? He'd been hurt by Marco, too. His brother lost a leg. But she was falling in love with him and before she fell any further, she had to know if he could accept what she'd done. She touched his shoulder with her lips and tasted salt.

"Marco and I were sixteen when we started dating. My mom wasn't crazy about him. She thought he was just another neighborhood punk. But I liked being courted by a semi-ruffian. It's the reformer in me. I was determined to remain pure because of what happened to my mom, and he … well, he was a typical teenage boy. The deeper I dug in my heels, the more he wanted me. So when my mom died just after graduation, he proposed. I had nowhere to go, and I thought I loved him, so I said yes. The rest is the usual story. A few years of passionate teenage sex, then we started to grow apart."

"No teenage pregnancy."

She squeezed him tighter. "We didn't try to prevent it. But in eight years of marriage not even one late period."

"Are you sorry?" He kissed her forehead.

"It was for the best, considering." That's what she told herself when loneliness overwhelmed her. "But his mother hated me as much for not giving her a grandchild as the rest."

"The rest?"

She stiffened in his arms, her heart began to boom. "I told you some of it already."

He released her and sat up. His eyes narrowed. "Some of it? What are you talking about?"

She sat, too, pulling up the blanket to shield her breasts. She couldn't look at him. "I did something that turned out very bad."

"What?"

"Marco called me early the day he died, the day that Adam was wounded. And we had a terrible fight." Tears sprang to her eyes. "He was so upset."

Jesse shifted away from her. "What did you fight about?"

"He wanted a divorce. He found someone new, and she was pregnant, and, I don't know, I just couldn't bear to let him go off and be happy and leave me behind. I cried, I begged, I screamed. I called his girlfriend names, called him names. But mostly I said no. Over and over again." She shook her head. "He was so angry. Then he went out on patrol and walked into a trap." A sob escaped from her throat. "And it's my fault. Everything. Marco would be alive, and Adam would be okay if it wasn't for me."

Jesse hissed one harsh word, "*Shit,*" before surging off the blanket and pulling on his boxers. Anger strained his voice. "That's the real reason you came to Cloud River and why you let Adam talk you making a scene at the supermarket."

Tears were streaming from her eyes. "I thought if I could help him maybe the guilt would go away."

Icy air pricked her skin, and she tried to wrap the blanket more tightly around her. But the cold came from the inside. She waited for him to say something. Anything. Yell at her or tell her how much he hated her. Anything.

"And did it?" He whispered the question softly.

She tried to dry her eyes, but the tears wouldn't stop. "Did what?"

"Did the guilt go away when you accused me of stealing your wallet?"

His eyes burned through the top of her head. She twisted the blanket around her and stood up. She couldn't look at him so she stared into the fire.

"I can't forgive myself." She dabbed at her eyes with the corner of the blanket.

"You used us."

"I didn't mean to."

"You didn't mean to act like some holier-than-thou angel descended on us in our dire need, preaching to me about family and love, giving Corrine and Adam false hope that they'd keep their house? And the entire time, it was all for you, wasn't it?"

"No!"

He took a step back. She waited. "I can't deal with this, with you, right now. I'm going to bunk in one of the bedrooms tonight. If you stay by the fire, you'll be warm enough." He spun away from her, hurried up the steps of the pit, and disappeared into the dark house.

Chapter Eighteen

Jesse latched a hatchet and saw to the back of Keystone's snowmobile and left the lodge before dawn. He headed out to check on the van and clear the tree off the road before the plows came through. Hacking and chopping under the bright, hard sun, he spent the day taking his frustration and pain out on the trunk of the Douglas fir.

He hated himself. Hated the way he'd treated Lin when she opened up to him. He should have pulled her in his arms and held her. Been a friend. *Had her back*. But all he'd felt was stupid. Hadn't he learned yet that everyone has an angle? That no one in the world cared what happened to an old hippie widow and her two pathetic sons?

As day dimmed into early evening, he rode slowly back to the lodge, his body sore and spent, his problems as large and fresh as ever. He rounded the last bend in the drive and braked the snowmobile so he could mentally prepare himself to face her. She'd been busy, too. The front steps and the driveway were cleared of snow. Smoke rose from the chimney.

Opening the snowmobile's throttle, he buzzed loudly past the house to warn her he'd returned, then parked the snowmobile behind the lodge. Above him a million stars blinked in the sky. He found the North Star, remembering when Robbie first showed it to him. He was seven, and he told Robbie he was going to be astronaut and fly up there someday. He'd wanted to fly ever since.

When he opened the back door, she was standing in the dimly lit kitchen, her back to him, stirring a pot on the stove. The mouth-watering aroma of chicken soup filled his nostrils. From the doorway, he studied her slender neck and the thick braid hanging between her shoulder blades. She looked small and vulnerable in the kitchen twilight.

He cleared his throat. "Hi."

She pulled a spoon through the broth. The rhythmic scrape echoed through the kitchen.

"Can we talk?"

She shrugged.

"Please, Lin."

"Why? You hate me, and I don't blame you. I hate myself more than you ever could."

He came closer. She smelled of soap and baby shampoo. "Come on." He laid his hands on her shoulders and pulled her back from the stove. "Let's sit down."

She nodded toward the doorway to the great room. "Not in there."

"Okay. Right here then."

She perched on the edge of a tall stool beside the breakfast bar. He took the stool beside her. His finger traced a thin white vein in the dark granite counter. It reminded him of the kitchen counter in the condo he shared with Adrienne. From where he sat right now, the life he led a year ago seemed like a distant dream.

"Well? Say what you have to say and get it over with."

"You threw me for a loop last night."

"I don't understand."

He tried to pull the corner of his mouth in a casual grin, but it refused. "You seem so honest and ... honorable, I guess. I didn't expect you to have an ulterior motive for helping the family. So when you told me why you'd really helped Corrine and Adam, I felt ... well, conned."

She stared at her fine-boned hands. He wanted to lift each one and kiss the palm then press her cool skin to his wind-burned cheeks. The silence between them stretched. Then she spoke, and the sadness that tinged each word fell on him like hard rain.

"I came to Cloud River to give Adam a check because I owed him. But that plan ended the minute I met all of you. You and Adam and Corrine are like my family."

"You still should have told us the truth. We deserved to know."

"I was nervous at first, then I started to care about you all so much, especially you. I was afraid you'd make me leave."

Wariness made him lean back from her. *Don't care about me.* He didn't want another helpless human being clinging to him. He wanted to be free. Free of Cloud River, free of Corrine's financial problems, free of his growing attraction for Lin, free of worry, free.

"I'm not worth caring about. Honest, Lin."

She shook her head, denying his bid for freedom. "Can you ever forgive me?" She whispered the words at her hands.

He wanted to exit this lodge right now and run all the way back to Denver even if he died of hypothermia. Because that's what it would take to save himself from the desire welling up inside him. But he was a soldier, and a good soldier knew when he'd been beaten. "You're a good person, Lin, and I'm sorry about the way I acted last night. I should never have doubted you. I know the help you've given Corrine, Adam, all of us has been genuine."

A shudder shook her body. "Are you forgiving me?"

In the great room, a log collapsed in the fireplace sending up a hiss of sparks. "None of this is your fault. Your husband is responsible for what happened to Adam, not you. Coming to us the way you did took courage." *Shit.* He was doomed.

"I lied."

"No. You came to help us, and you have. Adam and Corrine are much happier. You've given them that."

She lifted a hand and smooth down her braid. He itched to slip the elastic off and watch her shake it out the way she did last night. "I can't stop believing that Adam's injuries were my fault."

At least he could push some of her feelings onto someone else. "You're looking for something I can't give you."

"What?"

"Forgiveness. You must tell Adam what you told me."

She buried her face in her hands, and her body shuddered again. "I know you're right, but if he can't forgive me, I won't be able to bear it."

He pulled her arms until she standing between his legs, her head resting on his shoulder and his arms tightened securely around her waist. "You can't bear it now."

In the cold, semi-dark kitchen, he held her against him, steeling himself against her soft breasts pressed against his chest and the curve of her back beneath his hands. But his body was not so easily controlled, and as his erection grew, he tried to put space between their bodies.

He swallowed hard and tried not to sound strangled. "I really need a shower."

"Where were you all day?" She whispered the question into his neck. He inched her hips further away from him.

"Chopping up the tree that fell behind us on the highway. I cleared it off the road so the plows can go through." He stood up. Her head tipped down, and her eyes zeroed in on the bulge in his pants. "I guess I better make it a cold shower," he said.

"I'm not sorry about last night."

He was sinking fast. "Me either."

"Come on then." She slipped her hand into his and pulled him down a wide hall, through the master bedroom and into a glittering ivory-marble master bathroom. A glass-enclosed shower with two gold showerheads rose in the center of the room. She smiled at him. "A his and hers shower. What do you think?"

He thought he should shut this whole thing down before he was trapped forever. Then she pulled off her sweater and shimmied out of her jeans. She was wearing a black silk bra with lacy cups and a pair of panties cut high on her hips.

"Couldn't find a pair of cotton ones anywhere in the lodge." She reached behind her back and unhooked the bra.

He tried to smile, but groaned instead as the bra slid down her arms and landed on the floor at his feet. He reached out and ran a finger over each pale pink nipple.

She turned away from him. Perfectly round cheeks peeked out of the lacy black panties. "I'll start the water. You get undressed."

He did, struggling to keep his eyes on his shirt buttons as her sexy bottom swayed across the marble floor to the shower. The water was hot and the shower steamy when he joined her.

Pulling her under the showerhead with him, he turned her around and pressed her back to his chest, her bottom to his erection. The warm water rained down on their heads and streamed over their bodies. Her skin turned pink from the water and glistened. He reached behind him and groped for the bar of soap.

"Let me do your back, baby."

He soaped up his hands and slicked them down her back, reaching in front to coat her breasts with suds. He rubbed more soap on his hands and ran his palms down the curve of her back and over her round bottom. His hands slid lower, and he knelt on one knee behind her and slid his hands between her legs.

"Jess." She moaned his name in her soft voice. Her arms lifted and she leaned against the wall of the shower.

He played with her, enjoying the slickness of her sweet body. His finger dipped into her warm center. It contracted around him. His thumb rubbed over her nub. He kissed her waist and tops of her white cheeks.

She turned and looked down at him. Her eyes were dark with passion and need. "My turn."

He stood and handed her the soap, and tried to stand still as her light hands rubbed his chest, sliding behind him to caress his ass. His swollen manhood pressed against her and he reached for her. But she pulled away.

"Wait." She covered his erection with soap.

"That's it," he growled, knocking the soap out of her hand and pushing her against the wall of the shower. He lifted her up and she clung to him, arms wrapped around his shoulders, legs around his hips as he pushed into her. His self-control fled, his body was already pulsing. "I'm sorry. I can't wait."

"Me too." She threw her head back, and he felt her muscles tighten around his penis.

He was coming when he remembered. "Damn!" Her eyes flew open as he yanked her off him, and set her down on her feet. With a sigh of relief, he watched his seed spill into the stream of water and spin down the shower drain.

Chapter Nineteen

In the sun-drenched greenhouse, Linnea finished pruning the last tomato seedling and set the shears on the table. As she ducked under the trestle table to grab a bucket of compost, the door burst open. She jumped, cracking her head on the table. "Ouch."

"Jesse? Where are you?" A pair of hand-tooled cowboy boots with four-inch heels approached. They could only belong to one person. "Are you under the table, Jesse?"

Rolling her eyes, Linnea crawled out and stood. "Jesse's not here."

The tops of Ashley's breasts burst from a hot pink, v-neck sweater. A pair of tight jeans disappeared into her ridiculously impractical boots. Her cool blue eyes assessed Linnea, raking over her old tee shirt and landing on Corrine's rubber boots. "Duh. What happened to you guys anyway? No one knew where you were all week."

"It was four days, and Corrine and Adam knew where we were."

Ashley took a step closer. "Why are you such a bitch?"

She was sick of taking bullshit from Ashley. Besides Jesse was hers now—at least for the next few months—and the sooner Ashley knew, the better. "Why are *you* such a bitch? You walk in here like you own this place. It doesn't belong to you, at least not yet, and neither does Jesse."

"Oh. My. *God*. I get it now. You slept with him. That's what you guys were doing."

She hated Ashley Cooper and her designer clothes and her sports car and her manicured fingers and all her stupid money. Mostly, she hated that Ashley had slept with Jesse first, and she wasn't entirely sure Ashley couldn't get him back if she wanted to.

"It's none of your business where we went." That was lame.

"You did! How could you? He's mine, and *you* knew it." Ashley leaned back and swung one small palm at Linnea, hitting the side of her face.

Linnea staggered backward, pressing her hand against her stinging cheek. Her back hit the edge of the table. Anger washed over her. She swung back. A red hand-shaped stain spread over Ashley's cheekbone, and a mascara-blackened teardrop ran down her cheek.

"You bitch!" Ashley launched herself at Linnea, who hit the floor ass-first. Ashley landed on top of her, pushed her flat on her back and began pummeling her shoulders with her fists.

"Get off me!" Linnea swatted at Ashley's knuckles. "Stop it. Get off me." Ashley grabbed a hank of Linnea's hair and pulled it out of her ponytail. "Ow. That hurts."

"Good. It's what you deserve for trying to steal Jesse from me." She pulled Linnea's hair harder. "You'll never get him."

Linnea punched Ashley's arm. "Let go of my hair."

"I should cut it off. No guy would ever look at you again, you ugly skank." Ashley's free hand stretched toward the trestle and grabbed the pruning shears.

Linnea screamed. Her hand closed around Ashley's and she twisted it as hard as she could. The shears dropped to the cement with a loud clank.

It was Ashley's turn to scream. Unburdened of the shears, her hand swung at Linnea's face, but Linnea turned at the last minute and the blow glanced off her chin. The shears scraped across the floor, and when Linnea swung her head back to Ashley, they glinted in her hand. Grabbing Linnea's ponytail, she yanked it taut.

"Let's see how you look with a crew cut," Ashley sneered.

"No!" Linnea growled and tried to buck Ashley off her belly. Her hand pushed at Ashley's arm.

"Is there still time to place a bet?" It was Jesse.

Adam's voice piped up. "My money's on Ashley."

"Hmmm. Unfortunately, mine is too." Then Jesse lifted Ashley off Linnea. "Give me these before someone gets hurt." He gently unclenched Ashley's fingers and removed the shears from her hand.

Linnea scrambled to her feet, brushing bits of dirt and leaves off her jeans. Jesse looked at Linnea, then Ashley, then back at Linnea again. "What happened?"

Linnea glared at Ashley. "She attacked me."

Ashley slid her arms around Jesse's waist and pressed her breasts against his side. "How could you sleep with ponytail girl? I would have taken you back if I'd known you were that desperate."

Linnea's mouth formed an incredulous O. Her eyes flew to Jesse's.

He shook his head at her. *She's not worth it.* "I'm going to walk Ashley to her car. You stay here." One brow arched. "Didn't you have something you wanted to discuss with Adam?"

She widened her eyes in horror. "I can't—"

He nodded encouragingly. "You'll be fine." Then he marched Ashley outside.

Adam leaned against his crutches and smiled his sweet smile at her. If she could tear her leg off and give it to him, she'd do it without a second thought.

He lifted a crutch and pointed at a camp stool leaning against the leg of the table. "Pull up a seat. You look a little pale."

She grabbed two. "Why don't we both sit down?"

"Sure." He lowered himself onto the stool. "What's going on? This sounds serious."

She gazed down at her chapped hands and studied the dirt beneath her nails. She couldn't bear to look at him. "I don't expect you to forgive me, and—"

"Forgive you for what? Are you okay?"

She nodded. "I guess I better start at the beginning."

"Maybe you should cut to the chase."

"Yeah." She gulped and started over. "Well, the day Marco died, that morning he called from Afghanistan and asked me for a divorce. He'd just found out his girlfriend was pregnant. I refused. We had a horrible fight. He was so angry with me, Adam. Angrier than I've ever known him to be. That's why he didn't see the ambush coming. Because of me. My selfishness. Stubbornness."

She glanced up at him. A look of pure agony twisted his face. A lump settled in her throat. "That's why I chose you for the fund. I wanted to make things right for you so I would stop feeling so damn guilty all the time."

Silence descended over the greenhouse. The thin glass walls let in the far away sound of Ashley screaming at Jesse, then the yuk-yuk-yuk of a passing magpie. When Adam broke the silence, she jumped.

"I knew he was screwing around on you. We all did. He'd talk about her sometimes."

She hated asking, but she had to know. "Did he, uh, ever talk about me?"

He shrugged. "A little, maybe."

"It's okay. You don't have to say any more. Our marriage had been over for years, but he was Catholic, and I—" She stopped, unwilling to put her deepest fear into words.

"What?"

"I didn't want to be alone. I'm so sorry, Adam. If I could change places with you, I'd do it in a heartbeat."

"You don't know what you're saying."

"Tell me." If she could share his pain, maybe she could forgive herself.

He studied her for a moment. "Don't say anything to Corrine. She's been hurt enough."

"I won't."

"There's not much to tell really. One minute I was following Marco through a field of boulders, the next I was flat on my back and my ears were ringing. After the smoke cleared, I saw Marco a little ways off, lying on the ground, and I could tell he was dead. I looked down and saw my calf was mostly gone. Behind me, the other guys were taking fire, and I thought I was a dead man."

"It seemed like a million years passed before I heard the choppers coming for us. Then I passed out. When I woke up in the hospital, the nurse said, 'Don't worry, you're in Germany. You're safe.' As if that mattered." He paused. "Do you know what I did first?"

She shook her head.

"Maybe this isn't appropriate to say to my brother's girlfriend, but the first thing I did was check my, uh, junk. You know?"

Jesse's girlfriend? She didn't feel like it, but she nodded anyway. "Makes sense."

"I thought, as long as I'm still a man I can handle anything else. But that's not true. I couldn't save Corrine's home." A sob escaped from him, and he pinched his nose. "I felt so helpless when I wrote you."

"I'm sorry."

"Doesn't seem right to lose a leg and come home and lose our farm."

"It's not."

The silence settled over them again. "Have you ever been close to dying?"

"No."

"It changes your values. The things that used to matter to me like being rich or becoming a famous DJ seem worthless, and the things that I used to take for granted, like Corrine and Jesse, are worth more than all the gold in the world. I could never be angry with you. You've helped us."

"Adam, no—"

He held up his hand. "Just not in the way we expected. Not financially. But my mother is smiling again, and this morning I heard my brother whistling in the bathroom while he shaved. Whatever happens in the next few weeks, we're ready to face it now. That's worth something, too."

"Come on, Adam. Don't let me off so easily."

"If I could have my leg back, would I want it? Of course. But I can't, and I've been given other things in return." He studied her frowning face. "Okay. I forgive you. Not because you are guilty but because you need to hear it."

Linnea bowed her head and felt the pain of Marco's death drain away. But a small ache lingered like fumes from a dying fire. "I swear to you I'll spend the rest of my life trying to make the world a better place. And if you ever need anything from me—anything at all, not matter how big—you just have to ask."

"You've done enough for me. For us. It's time to let it go."

She swallowed. "I'll try." But she knew she couldn't.

He reached for his crutches and hoisted himself up. "Well, I better get ready for the station. City council votes next week on the church property."

His shoe brushed softly against the cement as he made his way to the door. When he got there, he stopped. "I heard you tip-toe out of my brother's bedroom this morning. What's the deal with you two?"

Her head snapped up. He was hunched over his crutches, watching her.

"We're just friends."

"With benefits?"

She shrugged. "Seems that way."

He nodded. "I suppose my brother is still carrying a big-ass torch for Lady Adrienne."

"That's her name?"

"Yeah. A ball-breaking witch."

"He says he'll never fall in love again."

Adam laughed. "That's Jess. Always in control." He winked at her. "My money's on you." He opened the door.

"Maybe Jesse is not the only McCormick man afraid of love."

He pivoted on his crutch and looked at her. A dark brow arched. "Yeah?"

"Hannah said to call her sometime."

A shadow crossed his face. "Touché."

With an aching heart, Linnea watched him swing his thin body across the yard and into the house.

Chapter Twenty

Linnea swung the Silverado into the driveway beneath a bright blanket of stars. But their ethereal beauty couldn't lift her spirits. Not tonight. The job interview in Greeley had gone disastrously well.

Her high-beams hit the garage. The white light rose until it exposed five words written in blotchy spray paint above the doors: *Last Warning Go Home Bitch.* She slammed the Silverado's brakes to the floor and her tires spun troughs in the gravel with harsh, popping sounds.

Someone in Cloud River really hated her. *Ashley?*

Her hand shook as she hit the automatic door lock. She slid low in her seat. Peering over the steering wheel, her eyes examined the bushes and trees for lurking shadows. Nothing stirred. She grabbed the gearshift. Before another brick came crashing through her window, she intended to be miles away. The gears ground together as she pulled the Silverado into reverse.

A light snapped on in the house, and Corrine passed in front of the window. Undulating shapes and colors appeared as the TV came to life. *How could she leave Corrine behind?* Linnea slipped the truck back into park, pulled out her cell, and punched in Jesse's number.

She hesitated, her finger hovering over the send button, and scanned the yard again. Nothing. If the vandal was gone, she'd be a cry-baby calling Jesse over a little spray paint. She'd been through this before. In the morning, they'd cover the ugly message with a new coat of paint, plus it would never happen again because she'd be gone soon.

She stuffed the phone back in her purse, turned off the engine, and killed the headlights. Then she waited, staying still in the darkness, praying her persecutor was gone. As she sat, she studied the path between her truck and the house. It seemed eerie and long in the muted light of the moon. Or maybe it was just jitters that made the play of light and dark seem sinister.

Ten minutes of dead silence passed. Slowly she eased up the lock and cracked open the door. It squeaked, and she winced before pressing it closed behind her. In the distance a coyote barked, then another and another. Then all was quiet again.

She crept around the back of the truck, staying close to the tailgate and keeping her head down. At the edge of the drive, the front walk shimmered in the light from the front window. The filigreed branch of an old oak etched a pattern in the light. She stepped out from the Silverado's shadow. Her feet crunched softly, slowly across the gravel.

The elongated shadow of a man came to life behind her. Strong arms closed around her chest, squeezing the breath out of her and pulled her off her feet. She managed one half-squeal of surprise before a rag was stuffed in her mouth.

"Shut up." The smell of damp wool filled her nostrils.

He dragged her across the gravel and pushed her face down against the hood of the Silverado. "Give me your hands."

She fought him, kicking at his legs, but he merely shoved her higher up on the hood and pinned her legs with his hips. Gloved hands grabbed her wrists and duct-taped them behind her back. "Stop kicking or I'll tape your ankles, too."

The rag was snaking down her throat. She tried to cough it up, but she gagged instead. Tears of panic and pain filled her eyes.

"Get out of Cloud River. Never contact the McCormicks again. This is your last warning. The next time I see your face around here, Corrine pays. Understand?"

She didn't move.

"Understand?" He pulled her up by the back of her jacket and banged her hard against the truck. Her breasts exploded with pain.

A scream vibrated in her throat but was swallowed by the gag.

Tears rolled down her cheek, and she nodded.

The deep, steady thrum of a car engine vibrated through the still night. The faint rumble approached, growing louder until it crystallized into the chug-chug of Jesse's van. Headlights pierced the darkness. Relief poured through her. *Hurry, Jesse. Please.*

Her attacker stepped away from her. She slid off the hood, landing flat on the ground. Her head hit a pointed rock, and a sharp pain knifed through the back of head. She gazed up at the black figure towering over her. He wore a ski mask.

"Don't forget. Next time it's Corrine." Then he sprinted across the front yard, around the side of house toward the greenhouses and the fields beyond.

The van roared into the driveway. Jesse burst from the vehicle, his boots hitting the gravel at the same time, and pounded toward her. He dropped to one knee and pulled her into a sitting position. "Are you okay?"

She nodded.

"Sorry." He pulled the rag out of her mouth. "Are you sure?"

"Yes." Her dry throat croaked the word.

"I'm going to leave you here for a few minutes. Okay?"

"Get him."

He leaned over and pecked her forehead before springing up and racing off in hot pursuit.

The gravel was sharp and bumpy. A rock poked her thigh, and she wiggled to push it out of the way, then she leaned wearily against the truck. The night air soaked through her jacket and into her bones. Her teeth chattered and the back of head throbbed. She tried to tuck her icy hands under her jacket, but the duct tape didn't have enough give.

"Please hurry, Jesse." She whispered the words over and over like a prayer until two dark figures appeared on the lawn. As they passed the front window, the light from inside illuminated Jesse dragging Kevin Burke behind him. Kevin's unmasked face was a mass of bruises. An angry-looking cut gaped over one eye.

When they reached the Silverado, Jesse released Kevin's arm. "Move and I call Teddy."

Kevin glowered at him.

Jesse slid his hands under Linnea's arms and hoisted her to her feet. "Turn around. Let's get this tape off you." His anger seemed to spill out of him as he unwound the duct tape from her wrists. "What a guy, Kev. You did a nice job immobilizing a five-and-a-half-foot woman." The tape loosened, and her arms released. "Did it make you feel big, asshole?" Jesse curled his fist and popped Kevin on the jaw.

Kevin spun around and hit the ground. He groaned and sat up, rubbing his jaw. "I said I'd tell you anything you want to know. What else do you want?"

"For starters, you can apologize to Lin."

"Sorry." He mumbled the word as he stood up.

The cold had seeped deep into her bones. She shivered. "Can we get out of the night air?"

"I'd rather have this conversation out here so we don't upset Corrine. Can you hold on a few minutes longer, Lin?" Jesse shrugged out of his coat and laid it over her shoulders.

She nodded and pulled his coat tightly around her. It was warm from his body and smelled like his skin, and it made her feel safe.

Jesse eyed Kevin. "What the hell is going on?"

Kevin's mangled face turned sullen. "Just doing my job."

"This is what the Coopers hired you to do?"

He shrugged one shoulder. "They said to scare Linnea away. That she was a trouble-maker. That's all I know."

"So you interpreted that to mean you should engage in criminal behavior."

Kevin's eyes widened, and he took a step back. "You said you wouldn't call Teddy if I cooperated."

"Answer me."

"The Coopers knew. The brick was my idea, but the rest, that was Ashley's and Mr. Cooper's."

"Why?"

He shuffled his feet. "I'm not sure."

Jesse grabbed the front of his shirt and yanked him closer. "Don't bullshit me."

Kevin's mouth formed a thin, hard line. He pulled away from Jesse and adjusted his shirt. "Why do you think, man? They want this place, and Corrine would probably have given in by now if *she*," he jerked his head at Linnea, "hadn't gotten you arrested so you couldn't leave the country."

Linnea looked around at the wide stretch of land that seemed to spread in all directions and the distant twinkle of Cloud River's lights. "It doesn't make sense. There are lots of other places to build houses."

Kevin shrugged again. "That's all I know."

Jesse followed Linnea's gaze. "Some of the land around here is government property, still…"

Kevin spoke up. "You know the Coopers. Once they set their sights on something, they don't take no for an answer."

Jesse nodded thoughtfully. "True."

In the distance, another coyote barked. The wind rustled the branches of the old oak. Linnea's legs wobbled, and she swayed against Jesse before straightening. She lifted her arm and touched the back of her head. Her fingers came away sticky with blood. "I better sit down."

Jesse glanced down at her fingers, then back up at Kevin. Kevin took a step backward and held up his hands. "Hey, man, I apologized. I answered your questions. That's all I can do."

She put her hand on Jesse's arm. "No more fighting. Please."

Jesse nodded. "Where's your car, Kev?"

"Down the road in the bushes."

"If I ever see you around here again or you ever get within a mile of Linnea, Teddy gets a call. And give Mr. Cooper a message for me."

"Sure. Whatever you want."

"If there is one more attack on Lin or this house, I'm coming down to their offices, and we are going to settle this. Man to man. And I'm bringing Teddy with me. Now get out of here."

Kevin nodded and half-limped, half-trotted down the driveway. He hustled up Canyon Road, over the rise, and disappeared.

Jesse slid his arm around her shoulder. "Come on. Let's get you inside."

*

Dressed in a worn flannel gown, Robbie's old robe wrapped snuggly around her, Linnea sipped green tea with Corrine at the kitchen table. In the front room, Jesse watched TV. Corrine yawned. "Well, I better go to bed before I fall asleep right here in the kitchen. Are you okay?"

Linnea took another sip of tea. "Fit as a fiddle. I'll be in soon."

Corrine tilted her head and studied her in a way that reminded Linnea of Adam. A hint of a smile danced around her lips. "Don't worry about me. Just make sure you get some rest tonight." Then she fluttered out of the kitchen calling out, "Good night, Jesse," as she passed through the front room.

Linnea put her cup in the sink and turned off the kitchen light. Jesse was lounging on the sofa, his feet propped on the coffee table. He held out an arm to her. "Come here." She did, sinking into the worn sofa cushion beside him. "What happened at your job interview at the day care center?"

She sighed. "They want me to start right away. One of the other assistants needs a roommate so that's no problem." He slid an arm around her shoulders and squeezed.

153

"That's great news."

"Maybe."

"What's wrong?"

"What about us? Will I see you?"

He turned her toward him. "Of course. As soon as you're settled, I'll drive up to see you."

She didn't want to be settled in Greeley. She wanted to stay here. "Why did you come home early?"

"I couldn't concentrate on the general ledger. Pictures of you in my bed kept flashing before my eyes."

Maybe he was falling in love with her. She loosened the robe and slid it off her shoulders before leaning into him. She kissed him lightly, and her eyes met his. *I love you.* But she couldn't say that. She'd agreed. *Friends.* "I just hope I don't end up falling in love with you."

His eyes softened into deep, green pools. "You won't. Think of me as a brief detour." He covered her mouth with his lips and kissed her until she couldn't breathe. When he pulled away, he gazed down at her granny gown. His fingers reached for her neck and slipped open the top button. "Did I ever tell you about my fantasy?"

She brushed his hair back from his forehead and felt her throat tighten. "Your fantasy? You only have one?"

He smiled into her eyes. "This is my newest one. It concerns you and this flannel nightgown."

"What happens in your fantasy?"

He reached in and loosened another button. "Guess."

Her body began to throb. "I have a better idea. Why don't we go to your room, and you can show me."

"Are you sure you're not too banged up?"

She planted a kiss at the corner of his mouth. "Open heart surgery couldn't keep me out of your bedroom tonight."

Chapter Twenty-One

The second Jesse walked into the house, he knew the end had come.

Corrine lay on the sofa with a damp cloth draped over her eyes and forehead. Her hand was pressed against her mouth as she tried to stem a flood of anguish. He closed the door behind him, and a loud sob escaped her lips.

Adam, eyes rimmed in red, sat nearby.

Lin knelt on the floor beside the sofa holding Corrine's hand. She looked up at him. Her wide gray eyes glistened with tears. "The bank's putting the property in foreclosure."

"When?"

"The fifteenth. Wednesday."

That gave him six days to put their affairs in order. He was relieved. The time for action was finally here. Tucked away in his little office in the greenhouse, an unsigned rental contract for a two-bedroom townhouse in Cloud River awaited his signature, and the brother-in-law of his old copilot had a job waiting for him in Denver flying the rich up to ski resorts. His modest salary would cover his rent, plus the townhouse. Once the dust settled, he would figure out a long-term plan.

Lin rose. "What are we going to do?"

This should be his moment of triumph. *I told you so.* But part of him was dying, too. This crazy house had been his only real home. "I found a place for Corrine and Adam in town. I'll sign the contract tomorrow."

Corrine popped up on the sofa. The washcloth flew off her head and landed on her knees. "I'm not selling this place to the Coopers."

His eyes slid to Lin. She shrugged helplessly.

"I mean it," said Corrine. "If we have to leave, at least find someone who respects God's green earth. I couldn't bear to see my life's work ripped apart for those monstrosities the Coopers call homes. Please, Jesse." Her dark eyes pleaded with him.

Another set of dark eyes turned to him. "At least we can try, can't we?" asked Adam.

Talk about a futile mission. But how could he say no? "I can't promise anything. But tomorrow morning I'll go down to the bank and talk to Jim Larsen. Maybe he'll give us a few more weeks to see if we can come up with a buyer. I'll post a notice on the organic websites tonight."

Corrine lay down again and pressed the wet cloth to her head. Adam went back to brooding. But Lin looked stricken.

She rose. "This is my fault. If I hadn't stopped you from meeting with Glenn Keystone, none of—" Her voice broke. She strode around the sofa and brushed past Jesse. "Excuse me."

"Where are you going?"

"Outside. I need time to think." She pulled Robbie's old sweater off a small bronze head and shrugged into it.

Think? That sounded dangerous. "I'll go with you."

She opened the front door then turned to him. "Your family needs you, and I want to be alone for a little while." Corrine emitted a loud wail. The door close behind Linnea.

It took him an hour and a half to get Corrine off the sofa. He tried to reason with her—*"It's inevitable."*—then he tried his West Point leadership skills—*"This is your chance to start a new life."*—he appealed to her emotions—*"We need you to be strong."* But Adam touched the nerve that finally got her up and moving again: maternal instincts.

"Is there anything to eat, Corrine?"

She sat up. "I forgot about dinner. You boys must be starving." She floated off to the kitchen, appearing both wan and determined at the same time.

He snatched up his coat. "I'm going to look for Lin. She's been gone for awhile, and it's getting dark."

The sky shimmered in the spring twilight. The earthy scent of damp, fertile ground filled the air. As he walked down the driveway toward the road, Jesse took a deep breath, trying to inhale a sense of well-being with the oxygen. But the future looked daunting, and this time next year, he would not be able to stand on his front lawn and breathe in sweet spring air.

He glanced up and down Canyon Road, but there was no sign of Lin. Maybe she'd retreated into one of the greenhouses to get warm. He turned back. The crazy turquoise house rose before him. As a kid, he'd hated this house. One day he begged Robbie to paint it white "like everyone else's house." His father looked hurt. *You worry too much, Jess. Enjoy life. That's what it's for.* He'd understood that Robbie would never change and began planning his escape to West Point.

"Are you okay?" Lin appeared from the side of the house.

"Sure."

She stood next to him and studied the house. "I was nervous the day I came, but when I topped the rise and saw this house, I felt this burst of optimism. Isn't that crazy?"

"Considering our current circumstances, yes." He curled his arm around her shoulder and drew her close to him. He'd need her comfort tonight. Then he stood with her in the gloaming, memorizing this last moment when he still had everything.

After awhile, she stirred and heaved a great sigh. "Even though my life sucks, deep down I've always believed that if I was good and did the right thing, I would be rewarded."

The tight rein he'd held on his emotions snapped. What was wrong with her? What was wrong with Corrine and Adam? He loosened his hold on her and stepped back.

"No, Lin. You get what you're willing to pay for. Period. You and Corrine and Adam think the universe owes you a good turn just because you're *good*. But so are eighty percent of the other people in this world. Do you see the kids in Afghanistan riding around in limousines and living in palaces?"

He should stop. Her eyes were gray saucers and her mouth an O of surprise. But his emotions rose like a tsunami and carried him away.

"You know what Afghanistan taught me?"

She shook her head.

"You have to bleed. That's right. You have to be willing to bleed to get what you want in this world. Doesn't matter if you're good or bad. The rule's the same for everyone."

She surprised him. "That's what I've been out here thinking about." She breathed the words, then dropped her head and stared at her boots. "I need to leave in the morning."

"The job in Greeley?" He asked the question softly, remorse already filling in behind the wave of despair.

"I got to get my life together." She tipped her head up and looked into his eyes. "I have something to say to you before I go."

He knew what was coming before she said it.

"I love you." The words sounded sad.

He couldn't deal with this right now. Maybe in a different situation, maybe if he was a better man, he'd love her back. She was an incredible woman. Her sweet, girlish exterior hid a big heart, full of determination and loyalty … and love. The innocent air she presented to the world also disguised a sexy, adventurous woman who surprised him nearly every night.

He pulled her hard against him. Her arms circled his waist and her warm head rested against his chest. His body stirred. If he didn't have to walk past Corrine and Adam, he'd have scooped her into his arms and carried her to his bed and made love to her until morning.

"This isn't a good time, Lin. After everything is settled, I'll drive up to Greeley and we can talk about this."

"Sure. That would be great." She released him. "I just wanted you to know before I left."

He tried to smile, but his mouth refused to turn up. "Let's go in. It's getting cold, and Corrine should have dinner ready soon."

Chapter Twenty-Two

Jesse folded and unfolded his legs. He draped his arms across his lap, then stuck his hands into his pants pockets. The worst part of being in the bank was the open waiting area that allowed everyone who walked in to stare at him. When his eyes met those of a little boy holding the hem of his mother's jacket with one hand and sucking his thumb with the other, Jesse picked up a brochure and pretended to study it.

"This is a waste of time," he muttered. He stared at a photo of an elderly couple embracing on a beach at sunset. His eyes wandered off the page. A bit of dust marred the polish on his black oxfords, and he bent to brush it off.

"Jesse?" Slightly stooped and wearing a rumpled pin-stripe suit, Jim Larsen stood at the doorway to his office.

Jesse jumped from his chair and shook Jim's hand. "Do you have a few minutes?"

"Sure. Come into my office."

Jesse straightened his tie and adjusted the pants of his Giorgio Armani charcoal suit. He hadn't worn it since he'd been home, and he'd lost weight this past year. This morning when he dressed, he'd tightened the alligator belt—like the suit, a gift from Adrienne—to the last hole, and he still needed to hitch up his pants every few minutes.

Jim closed the door and sat down behind his gleaming desk. "Have a seat, Jess. Can I get you some coffee?"

"I'm good." Jesse lowered himself into a hard chair in front of the desk. "I guess you know about our situation."

"Your father was not only a customer, he was a friend. I had enormous respect for him. A better man didn't exist anywhere on the planet. But there's nothing I can do for you."

"I'm not here asking for a second chance. I'm just asking for a few extra weeks so my mother can find a buyer who will continue the organics tradition my father worked for all his life."

Jim's expression grew sad. "You know I would if it were possible."

"Come on, Jim. For my father's sake you can't give my mother a little more time? She'd be grateful for even one week." He hated begging, but if he could bargain even seven extra days out of the bank for Corrine, he'd feel better.

Jim sighed and rolled his chair closer to his desk. He leaned toward Jesse and spoke softly. "Your father's years on the Village Council and your mother's kindness to those in need and the sacrifice you and your brother made for the country..." He looked away for a moment. "I shouldn't be telling you this, but your family deserves to know the truth."

Jesse's foot began to tap softly on the nubby, money-green carpet. At least he'd have something to bring home. "I promise to be discreet."

"The bank's in a little trouble. That's why I can't push your foreclosure date out."

"Trouble?"

Jim nodded. "The housing bubble caught the Coopers with their pants down. They owe us almost ten million."

Jesse's foot stopped tapping. How could the Coopers be planning a new development if they were broke? Where was the money for the farm coming from? "I'm surprised."

Jim nodded. "We've kept everything quiet at their request. They've promised us four million by May first, but we haven't seen any pick-up in their business. We're probably going to be forced to eat the entire ten mil come the first of the month." He twiddled his thumbs as he gazed across the desk at Jesse. "We're trying to clean up our books as much as we can before then."

May first, Jess, if you want a decent price for that pile of shit you live in.

His body suddenly felt weightless. He straightened. Ashley wasn't going to develop the farm. She'd lied to them, and so, he suspected, had Kevin. The Coopers wanted the farm because it was worth four million dollars! Probably more since Kevin was apparently going to get a cut of the proceeds. Was Corrine sitting on a gusher? Maybe a vein of gold snaked across their fields. Whatever it was, he intended to find out. If Ashley wouldn't tell him, he'd beat it out of Kevin. Then again, maybe he'd beat Kevin just for the hell of it.

"I appreciate your honesty. We're all facing tough times."

The thumb-twiddling stopped. "Thanks. If there's anything I can do to ease Corrine through this difficult time ..."

You already have. Jesse stood up. "I've taken enough of your time. Thanks again for confiding in me."

Jim walked with him to the door and shook his hand. "Sorry, Jess."

"I appreciate your candor. Sorry about the ten million."

*

The campaign office was unusually quiet for a Friday morning, but Linnea was glad for the privacy. Ken was here. That's all that mattered.

He sat behind his desk writing notes into a leather-bound portfolio in his loopy, elegant handwriting. He looked up when her shadow crossed his desk.

"Well." He pulled off his reading glasses. "That didn't take long. Close the door and have a seat."

She felt her panic bleed away along with her repulsion. Jesse wouldn't be afraid, and neither would she. She lowered herself into one of his plush, silk-upholstered guest chairs. Then she got down to business. "What do you want?"

Ken leaned back in his gleaming leather chair and studied her. "Have you made up your mind?"

"Yes."

"No matter what I ask, you're going to marry me."

"Yes."

He opened his credenza. A small, gun-metal gray safe hunkered behind the mahogany door. He spun the combination lock back and forth until it swung open, then pulled out a manila envelope. "In my position, one can't be too careful. This is a confidentiality agreement." He laid a legal document on the desk in front of her. "Sign it. Basically it says you agree to keep anything you learn about my personal life confidential. No books, media interviews, et cetera."

She should be frightened out of her mind, but she felt nothing. If he wanted to beat her every night, then she would endure it. She would bleed, and in return he would give her what she asked for. A spark of resolve flared inside her. If he didn't, *he* would bleed. She would make sure of it. She pressed her finger tips against the paper, slid it close and signed it.

He put the document in the safe. The heavy door swung shut and clicked.

His light blue eyes studied her for a moment. With a deep breath, he leaned forward. "You need to understand how difficult it is for me to discuss this, but in order to fulfill the next phase of my career, I must trust you. From the look on your face, I gather you want something, too. Hopefully that will ensure an enduring partnership for us both."

"Of course." *Call it whatever you want. Just get to the point.*

"I need a beard."

He'd managed to surprise her. "A beard?"

One perfectly shaped, winged brow arched. "A woman who is my wife everywhere but in the bedroom."

"But you have kids and—"

He cut her off. "Let's just say men are my preference."

"But why did you grab—"

He smiled tightly. "You must be obedient until you learn the rules of Washington. I just wanted to be sure you were manageable."

"That's why you chose me. Because I was manageable." Strangely, relief warmed her body and loosened her tense muscles. No sex.

"I chose you because you're young and beautiful, and you have a certain vulnerability that draws people in. Plus—and this is a big plus—you have no family, which means no embarrassing skeletons jumping out of the closet in the middle of a campaign, and no nosy mother-in-law poking around in my life."

"I see." She would live the rest of her life without a man, but she'd had Jesse. Her memories would have to carry her through. Considering her track record with relationships maybe it was better this way.

"Did your G.I. Joe dump you?"

"We were just friends."

"That sounds like a yes." He opened his desk drawer and pulled out a pale blue Tiffany's box. "Too bad. You have great taste in men." He lifted a garish diamond ring out of the box. The solitaire was larger than the Rock of Gibraltar and the band was encrusted with glittering diamond baguettes. He slid it on her finger. "Be ready to leave this afternoon for Hawaii. We'll have a destination wedding."

"What about your side of the bargain?"

"Ah, yes. What do you want from me?"

"Set up a trust for Corrine so she can live in her house for the rest of her life."

"Okay."

"Before we leave for Hawaii."

He nodded. "Is that it?"

She leaned forward. "Does that confidentiality agreement work both ways?"

Chapter Twenty-Three

The Cooper Construction Building was quiet when Jesse walked in. A middle-aged woman with bleach-blond hair and a gravely voice sat at the front desk examining her nail polish as she chattered on a cell phone. She didn't look up when he approached her.

"Excuse me," he said.

She ignored him.

A mixture of exhilaration and fury coursed through him. He was a steam engine, throttle opened wide, barreling down the tracks. "Excuse me, ma'am."

She looked up at him and scowled.

He reached across the desk and pulled the phone out of her hand.

"Hey!" She made a grab for it, but he held it high, just out of her reach.

"Is Ashley Cooper here?"

"Not yet."

"How about Kevin Burke?"

Her eyes narrowed. "Do you have an appointment?"

"No."

"Then you can't—"

"I can."

She made a grabbed for the phone. "I'll call the police."

He held it higher. "I bet I find Kevin first." He walked toward the elevator.

"My phone!" Her croak echoed through the deserted reception area. He pressed the plastic button beside the elevator and watched it light. Ashley's office was on the second floor. Her accessory in crime was no doubt close by. "My phone. Give it back."

The elevator doors opened. "Tell me where he is." He stepped into the elevator. "Well?"

"Second floor. Turn right. He's halfway down. His name's on the door."

The elevator doors began to close. "Catch." He tossed the phone to her.

Feet up, chair tilted back, Kevin was chatting on his phone. When he saw Jesse standing in the doorway, he put the receiver down and stood. Jesse closed the door.

"What do you want?" Kevin's dark eyes studied him warily.

Jesse's hands curled into fists. "Tell me what the Coopers want from us."

Kevin smoothed the nervous creases streaking across his forehead and primly pressed his lips together. But he couldn't hide the fear in his eyes. Jesse took a step forward.

"I told you everything I know the other night."

"You neglected to tell us why the Coopers are so hot for Corrine's property."

"Come on. I told you already—"

Jesse grabbed a fistful of Kevin's crisp cotton shirt. He yanked him close. "You tell me the truth, or I call Teddy Scripps."

Kevin shook his head sadly and tried to look regretful, but his eyes didn't meet Jesse's. "I mean it. I don't know."

Jesse twisted Kevin's shirt until it ripped. "I make the phone call on five. One, two." He gave Kevin's shirt another vicious twist. "What's the mandatory sentence for assault with a deadly weapon? Three, four."

"It was a brick."

"Exactly. Five." Jesse released the shirt and shoved Kevin against the wall. He hit the plasterboard with a dull thud and staggered to regain his footing.

Jesse pulled out his phone and hit Teddy's number.

"Come on, Jess. Be reasonable."

Jesse held the phone to his ear. "It's ringing." Kevin went still. Teddy came on the line. "Hey, Teddy. It's Jess. Look, I—"

"No." Kevin whispered the word. "I'll tell you."

"—was wondering if you had time for a beer tonight."

To his relief, Teddy declined. Jesse hung up. "I'm waiting."

Kevin's face crumpled. "It's the statues."

"The statues of the kids?"

He nodded. "They're by a famous artist or something. Ashley saw one in a gallery in New York last year. That's how she figured it out. She has a buyer lined up as soon as Corrine signs the papers."

Jesse could barely breathe. His feet were rooted to the carpet, his arms frozen at his sides while he tried to get his head around Kevin's words. Corrine was going to keep her home. His own future opened with possibility again. He felt light-headed and giddy with relief.

Kevin's door banged open. "Irma said that someone was looking—" Ashley stared at Kevin's disheveled figure. Her eyes met Jesse. "Oh, my god. What just happened?"

The corner of his mouth crooked up. "Guess."

Her eyes flashed angrily. "They're mine!"

"They're Corrine's."

"Ooooh, I *hate* you. I went to New York. I discovered them. I did the research. I found the buyers. What did Corrine do to deserve the money? Nothing. I *earned* those."

He was so pumped with happiness, he couldn't even find the energy to be pissed at her. Maybe Lin was right. Maybe good things did happen to good people. You just had to be a little patient. "They belong to Corrine, and you tried to cheat her out of them."

Ashley stamped her foot. "That bitch! This is her fault. If she hadn't stuck her stupid nose into our business, none of this would be happening. I'm going to rip her freaking hair out."

He turned toward the door.

Ashley grabbed the sleeve of his coat. "What am I supposed to do, Jess? We need that money."

The Coopers would rise again. Of that he was sure. In the meantime, it was the McCormicks' turn to live the high life for a change. He reached into his suit coat and pulled out the lease for the condo and tossed it to Ashley. It landed at her feet. "Here."

Her eyes gleamed suspiciously, but she stooped down and picked it up. "What it is?"

"A lease for the condo where Corrine was going to live the rest of her life after you fleeced her."

"Jesse!" His name sounded like the screech of a dying animal.

He strode out of the office, and as he hit the hallway Ashley's voice rose again. "You stupid idiot, Kevin. You're *fired*."

Music to his ears.

*

The van roared into the driveway triumphantly. As soon as he told Corrine and Adam the good news, he was going straight up to Greeley and Lin. She was only one he wanted to be with, the only one he wanted to share this amazing moment with. He'd surprise her. Maybe stop on the way and pick up roses—red ones—and a bottle of champagne. Something good, like the stuff he used to drink with Adrienne. He could barely get his head around it, but Ashley was right. Lin was the reason for their good fortune.

He was barely out of the van when the front door swung open, and Corrine flew out. She was sobbing as she stumbled toward him. She fell into his arms and buried her head in his jacket. Adam swung out of the house behind her. His face was grim.

"What happened?"

Corrine lifted her head. "The bank called." She started wailing again and dropped her head against his chest.

He turned to Adam. "What is going on?"

"Like she said, the bank called. The loan was paid off this morning, and a trust fund was set up for Corrine."

Jesse frowned. "I don't understand."

"Yeah, I didn't either until Jim said that Senator Klein's fiancée made the arrangements."

Chapter Twenty-Four

Peering through the clouds, Mitty watched greening patchwork fields roll by. The farmland below was coming to life. It was spring. She'd been in the hospital a long, long time. After her meeting with The Possum, a bug had burrowed deep into her lungs, and her days had been reduced to a struggle for life. During moments of clarity, she prayed for more time to find Murphy's daughter. Now, thanks to or in spite of The Possum, who'd proved to be a slow-witted investigator, she had the name of a girl she suspected was her niece, the savior of Basinger Industries—although it was possible that Mitty's conceit was born of the drugs they were pouring into her.

She'd never been to Denver, but when the plane touched down, she liked how the mountains rose in the distance like a flexed bicep. The limo drove her straight from the airport into downtown. It was noon, and the sidewalks were full. She scanned every female face she passed, hoping to spot Murphy's daughter.

At Senator Klein's headquarters, the open campaign office was a hive of activity, and her eyes started on one side of the room and carefully examined each young face. But none belonged to the girl in the magazine. She stopped a young man hurrying past with a stack of posters in his arms. "Excuse me, I'm looking for Linnea Reyes. Is she here?"

He shook his head. "Gone. She and the senator are leaving this afternoon for Hawaii. They're getting married."

She didn't know if the answer to her next question would yield good news or bad, but she asked anyway. "Can I get in touch with her quickly? I'm … family. I need to meet with her before she leaves."

*

Linnea folded the last of her meager wardrobe into the canvas bag and sighed. Two pairs of worn jeans, her denim skirt, a few tee shirts, the green shirt she bought with Corrine … Jesse had loved that shirt. But the senator—Ken—wouldn't approve of a cheap shirt from the discount store. She'd probably never wear it again, at least not in public. He'd already ordered an "appropriate" wedding gown and sent over a silk dress for the trip.

She held the dress up to her shoulders and studied herself in the mirror. The gray eyes gazing back at her were clear and steady. This was the right thing to do. The pain of walking away from Jesse was softened by the fading away of the guilt she'd carried for so long. The McCormicks were safe thanks to her.

Dropping the dress over her head, she let it settle on her body and turned to inspect her profile. Her hand brushed across her belly. It was still flat, but a baby was growing inside. Jesse's baby. Maybe if things had been different, she would have told him. Maybe not. He didn't love her. He loved the general's daughter and his freedom. Ken would be the baby's father, at least in name.

Ken. She'd have to learn to please him. Not in the bedroom, of course, for which she was grateful, but everywhere else. And she'd have to learn to live without Jesse and the McCormick's. The only real family she'd ever known. Would ever know.

Someone knocked on the apartment door. It was probably Gary with the limo. She pulled the canvas bag off the bed and hauled it to the front hall. He could take it downstairs while she brushed her hair and dabbed on some lipstick. She opened the door, and her breath caught. Her mother, or a woman who looked exactly like her, stood on the threshold.

"Mom?" The word slipped out of her mouth with a kind of wonder.

"Linnea Reyes?" The woman even sounded like her mother.

Linnea nodded.

"I'm Mitty Basinger. Your aunt." Mitty Basinger's eyes narrowed. "I assume from your expression you weren't aware your mother had a twin sister."

Chapter Twenty-Five

May came in sunny and hot. A welcome relief from April when each day brought thick black clouds, endless drizzle, and constant thoughts of Lin. The clouds suited his mood, but he was grateful for the bright sun. Maybe it would drive away the lingering gloom inside him.

Less than a week after Lin left, he'd fled Cloud River, angry at himself for letting another woman get under his skin and determined to put her out of his mind. He'd taken the job with the private airline while he debated what to do with his life. But memories of Lin followed him everywhere. *Where was she?* He'd never seen a wedding announcement in the paper, and then a week ago there'd been a photo of the senator in the *Post* with a woman who looked a bit like Linnea. But as for Linnea herself, it was as if—her rescue of the McCormicks complete—she'd sprouted wings and flown away.

Wiping beads of sweat off his forehead, he crouched on the tarmac inspecting a Cessna 525 jet. Behind him, the doors to the empty hangar yawned wide. His boss and the other pilot were flying guests to Lake Tahoe and Durango.

The light click of a woman's heels on the tarmac grew louder and closer. His passenger for Vail. She'd requested Jesse when she reserved the plane.

"Hi, Jess."

He turned slowly. Endless legs in tight white jeans. Gold sandals with mile-high heels strapped to a pair of tanned feet. He tilted his head up. She'd tied the tails of a soft mint-green blouse around her midriff, baring a perfectly curved waist. A diamond navel ring shimmered in the sun. She flipped her sun-streaked brown hair behind her shoulder with slender fingers manicured in pearly pink. Her dark eyes smiled at him.

He straightened. "Adrienne." Her name came out like a croak.

She leaned into him and kissed his cheek. The scent of her lemony perfume filled his nostrils. "Surprised?"

He stuck his hands in his back pocket and tried to look relaxed. "Yeah. What brings you to Colorado?"

A light breeze kicked up, and her dark hair lifted. She reached behind her head and pulled the shiny mane into a hand-held ponytail. Then she gazed at him through her long lashes. "I thought maybe we could talk. I heard things turned around for you."

His heart skipped a beat. "Sure." He waved a hand toward the hangar. "The office is air-conditioned. We can talk in there."

She threw back her head and laughed. The sound echoed over the hot tarmac like a bright bell. She stepped closer to him and slipped her arm through his. "I have a better idea. There are reservations in my name at The Sebastian in Vail. Let's fly up together. We can have a quiet dinner and catch up over a glass of wine and a great steak." Her wide eyes lifted. "What do you think?"

He frowned at her. This neat little scenario showed all the earmarks of one of Adrienne's battle plans. "What gives?"

Her bravado disappeared. "I miss you, Jess."

Conflicting emotions tumbled through him. The woman he'd dreamed about for over a year had just flown halfway across the country to visit him. She was also the woman who threw him out like yesterday's trash at the lowest point in his life. He stalled her. "I expected you to be married or at least dating someone by now."

Her eyes met his and her shimmering pink lips curved into a rueful smile. "You're hard to forget."

"So I've heard."

She didn't laugh. Dark eyes, luminous with emotion, studied him. "Was it a mistake for me to come?"

He shook his head. "I don't know." Over her right shoulder, the Rockies pushed toward the sky. He couldn't look at them without seeing Lin. His gaze slid back to Adrienne's face. "Dinner in Vail sounds good."

Relief sparkled in her eyes and colored her cheeks.

Desire stirred in him. "Do you have any luggage?"

She pointed toward the hangar at a large bag emblazoned with a designer logo. "Is there someone who can load it on the airplane?"

He raised an eyebrow. "Yeah. Me." Leaning into her, he bussed her cheek. "It's a jet not an airplane."

Chapter Twenty-Six

*The thickness of the pipeline metal is five-hundredths of an inch and
…*

This was so boring. Linnea's eyes rolled up in her head, her head fell forward, and her nose hit the edge of her desk.

"Ouch." She rubbed the bridge of her nose. Everything about being pregnant was amazing, except the afternoon slump. What she wouldn't give right now for a mug of Corrine's ginseng tea.

"Linnea!" Julian's voice blasted out of the intercom on her desk. She jumped, and the button on the waistband of her skirt popped off.

"Linnea! Where are you? Answer me."

She hated her cousin. Everything about him was heavy and revolting—his body, his breath, his jowls, his sweaty skin, his thick voice, his wrinkled suits. When his disapproving glare landed on her, it was like a herd of elephants was sitting on her chest.

"In my office. Five doors down from yours by the way."

"I've been waiting since Monday for you to finish the agenda for the board meeting."

"I'm still working on it." She'd never even been to a business meeting, much less run one. She wasn't even sure what Basinger Industries did, except that it was something industrial.

"I need the agenda *now*! The board will be in town next week."

"You'll have it tomorrow."

"I don't understand why Mitty wanted you to do it. Clearly you're incompetent."

"Thanks loads." She took a deep breath to shore up her courage and plunged in. "I do have one item I'd like to bring up."

"What?" He sounded disinterested.

"Aunt Mitty told me that the Basinger Foundation hasn't dispersed any funds in the three years since she got sick. I'd like activate it again. Focus on helping veterans get back on their feet."

"Have you lost your mind? You're supposed to be boning up on the pipeline we *are* acquiring and preparing to address a myriad of other important issues. Get your head out of the clouds, Linnea, and get to work." His voice blasted through the intercom and made her ears ring. "If you worked for me, I'd fire you."

Aunt Mitty told her not to show Julian any weakness. "If *you* worked for *me, I'd* fire you."

Of course, if she fired Julian, there'd be no one at the board meeting familiar with the pipeline since she fell asleep every time she looked at the report. Why couldn't they buy something she knew about like an organic farm or a daycare center?

The intercom went dead, but not before he growled, "Bitch."

"Bastard." She muttered the word into the dead microphone.

Restless, she stood up, pulled her blouse out of her skirt to hide her gaping waistband, slipped off her heels, and padded over to the door. The hushed tones of Basinger executives drifted down the deserted corridor from open doors. What she wouldn't do to see a friendly face. Maybe she'd buy a goldfish for her office.

The thick report sitting on her desk mocked her. When Aunt Mitty asked for her help, Linnea had pictured something along the lines of running errands and walking the dog. But she'd fallen in love with her funny, irreverent aunt who'd rescued her from a life as Ken's slave by paying him back every penny he'd given the McCormicks then opening her home to Linnea and the baby. More than anything, Linnea wanted to help Aunt Mitty keep Basinger Industries out of Julian's hands … if she could just concentrate.

Her gaze drifted around her office, flicking over teak furniture, a soft leather sofa and chairs, a thick Persian carpet, and bird prints in gilded frames. It was larger than her last apartment, and she'd trade it all away just to see Jesse again.

It had been nearly four months since she left Cloud River, and her love for him seemed to deepen with the weeks of separation. She'd wanted him to have his freedom, but what if she was making a mistake? What if he'd be pleased about the baby? Maybe it was time to feel Corrine out on what Jesse was up to.

She pulled out her cell.

Corrine's phone rang four times as Linnea padded back to her desk, wriggling her tortured toes in the soft wool carpet. Rounding the Olympic-size desk, doubts began to fill her. Her finger hovered over the disconnect button.

"Linnea!" Corrine squealed her name. "Is it really you?"

"Yeah, it's me." She plopped into her leather chair and leaned back. A smile curved her lips. It was wonderful to hear Corrine's voice.

"Are you okay?"

"Great."

"I saw a picture of the senator in the *Post* with a new fiancée. What happened to you?"

"My aunt found me. I'm living with her in Chicago. She's great. Really funny and nice. How are you?"

"Wondering when you'll come back. Everything around here is green, and my tea garden is planted. I bought a little bench for the middle. We can sit and watch the bees and butterflies flitting around the flowers."

It sounded like heaven. She studied her waist again. "I'm helping my aunt with her company so I don't have much time. Besides, I don't want to bother Jesse."

"You won't. He left about a week after you. Moved to Denver."

"What's he up to?"

"I don't want to upset you."

Her throat went dry. "It's fine. Things weren't going to work out between Jesse and me."

"If you're sure."

"Absolutely." She was such a liar.

"Adrienne came back to him. She found out we're not on the verge of ruin." Corrine sounded disgusted. "First Ashley, now Adrienne again. When is he going to get some common sense?"

The muscles in Linnea's face tightened, and her throat ached with tears.

"Are you okay?" asked Corrine.

"I … I'm sure he'll be very happy. I know he really loved her." She was definitely getting a goldfish.

Chapter Twenty-Seven

As quietly as possible, Jesse slid his key into the front door and slipped into the dark living room.

"You're late." Adrienne's soft, raspy voice had an edge to it.

Exhaustion squeezed the back of his neck. Dry lightning had grounded his plane in Sundance until nearly eleven o'clock. He flipped the light switch and fought to keep his eyes open. Adrienne was curled on the sofa, sleepy-eyed, hair tousled, wrapped in a soft gray blanket. She never waited up for him. He was suddenly wide awake.

"You should be asleep," he said.

She smiled and rubbed her eyes. "I couldn't sleep until I told you the news."

"News" usually meant she'd done something he wasn't going to like. He tossed his keys on the wooden stand beside the door—one of Adrienne's 'little touches' as she called her incessant decorating—and sat down beside her on the sofa.

"It's the best. Unbelievable. Dad's coming to visit."

"You moved in five weeks ago. Does he miss you already?"

She scooted closer to him, and when he didn't draw her to him, she lifted his arm and snuggled underneath. The blanket fell open long enough for him to glimpse a rosy nipple. Then it was gone as she pulled the blanket tight across her shoulders.

Adrienne planted a soft kiss on his jaw. "I thought you liked my father." Her voice vibrated against his chest. The edge of the blanket fell open again. He reached down and pressed it back into place.

"I do. Look, I'm beat. Can we talk in the morning?"

Her voice turned pouty. "Come on, Jesse. I've been alone in your stuffy little apartment all day while you've been out playing with your stupid airplane—excuse me—jet. Can't you spare ten minutes out of your busy day for me?"

He scowled at the hulking new cupboard….no, not a cupboard, something else. *Armoire.* That's what she called it. It took up half the living room, and he'd been forced to move his big screen into the bedroom and buy a new TV to fit in the armoire. It was the size of a postage stamp. He willed himself to persevere. "Sorry."

She snuggled in closer. "Dad is so excited that we're back together."

"Why? I'm an underpaid rent-a-pilot."

"Not for long. He wants to talk to you about getting a new commission. Wouldn't that be great? Everything would be back to normal."

He straightened up and retrieved his arm. "Dammit, Adrienne."

Her dark eyes filled with tears. Her chin began to quiver. "Why are you mad at me?"

"Are you kidding me? You have no right to make decisions about my life without discussing it with me first."

"I thought you'd be so happy to get out of this stupid town. And I wanted to surprise you."

What was he supposed to say to that? *Thank you?* A wave of fatigue washed over him, taking his anger with it. He was an asshole, an ungrateful brute of an asshole, but a justified asshole, too. He pulled himself together. "It's late. Why don't we get some sleep? We can sort things out tomorrow."

"If you insist." She sounded pleased as she followed him into the bedroom, but he was too tired to wonder why.

He undressed and lay down beside her, but he didn't reach for her.

"Are you still a little bit mad at me?" she asked in a small voice.

"Nah. Just tired. Go to sleep."

Her breathing grew deep and even, but his fatigue had fled. He lay in the dark, eyes wide open, gazing at the ceiling. What was wrong with him? He should be happy. Thrilled. Everything he lost last year was within his reach again.

Maybe it was the way she sprung it on him. He probably just needed time to get his head around his good fortune. Still, he couldn't relax, and by the time he finally drifted off, the first rays of the sun were peeking over the eastern horizon.

*

Jesse woke to bright sunshine. Cracking open one bleary eye, he checked the bedside clock. Almost ten. He groaned and stretched his back. Then he pulled on a pair of cargo shorts and went in search of coffee.

He shuffled into the living room, yawning and scratching his belly, to discover General Wrightwood, Adrienne's father, comfortably installed on the sofa.

Jesse's feet ground to a halt, and his shoulders squared. "Sir."

"How are you, Jesse?" General Wrightwood was dressed in civilian clothes—khakis pressed to knife-edge sharpness and a top-of-the-line golf shirt—but no one would ever mistake him for a regular guy. The *New York Times* rested on his lap.

"I'm fine, sir." Jesse rolled his shoulders and tried to relax. He was a civilian now.

"This isn't an official visit. 'Sir' isn't necessary."

"Yes, um, Bill."

General Wrightwood smiled, but his pale eyes pierced Jesse. "Adrienne told me that she'd mentioned the purpose of my visit to you last night."

Jesse glanced down at his bare feet. *He was going to kill Adrienne.* "I wasn't expecting you this morning. Give me ten minutes to wash up and put on a clean shirt and some shoes."

The general didn't look pleased. "I have another appointment."

In Denver? Jesse doubted it. But he'd known Adrienne long

enough to recognize a Wrightwood maneuver when he heard one. "Sorry, sir." He turned and fled the room, banging the bedroom door behind him.

He shaved, combed his hair, and swished mouthwash vigorously from cheek-to-cheek, hoping the sharp sting of the alcohol would wake him up. He studied himself in the bathroom mirror, staring into his own eyes. Who was staring back at him? Poking his head in his closet, he glanced over the row of expensive new shirts on overpriced, matching hangers and pulled out one of his old polos.

The general closed the paper as soon as Jesse reappeared. "Sit down." He waved at the seat beside him on the sofa.

Jesse pulled up a chair on the other side of the coffee table.

The newspaper rustled as the general set it aside and picked up a framed photo of Jesse and Adrienne.

"Great picture of you two."

When was it taken? He couldn't remember exactly. He was wearing his green service uniform, belt and shoes shined, medals and insignia gleaming, his expression serious and proud. At his side was Adrienne in a strapless gold gown, looking like a Greek goddess.

"The perfect couple. That's what people used to say."

"Yes, sir."

"Cut out the 'sir' stuff." The general chuckled. "That's an order."

"Sorry, Bill."

"Back then, I expected you and Adrienne to be married by now and on your way to producing the first Wrightwood grandchild."

"You mean McCormick." He watched the General set the picture on the table and flick a bit of dust off the glass before looking at him.

"I beg your pardon?"

"McCormick." When the General looked confused, he clarified. "All of my children—if and when I have them—will be McCormicks."

The General treated him to a hearty, ersatz laugh. "Of course. I just meant that Adrienne is my only child so her children will be my heirs." He dismissed the topic with a wave of his hand. "You and Adrienne can hash out the details on names between yourselves."

Jesse cocked his head and eyed the man. "It could be awhile. We've only been back together a month or so."

"Nonsense. Adrienne loves you. She tells me she's never been happier. That's all that counts. We'll get your commission back, start the paperwork for your promotion ..." He stopped. "You'll have to work hard for a couple years. Your stock went down when you walked out. But I have faith in you. You won't let us down again."

Jesse dropped his head. How many times had he ached for Adrienne and his army career? How often had he dreamed of getting back everything he lost until he almost exploded with yearning? Now it was his for the taking. But he couldn't pull the trigger. "I appreciate the offer, Bill, but I need time to think this through. It's a big step."

The general frowned at Jesse. "Is there a problem?"

"I want to discuss this with Adrienne. After all, this concerns her."

On cue, Adrienne stepped out of the kitchen, a soldier's wet dream in a halter top and tiny white tennis skirt. A pale blue scarf fluttered in her dark hair. "Did I hear my name?"

Jesse rose slowly to his feet. His head turned from daughter to father, back to daughter again. "What the hell is going on, Adrienne?"

Her eyes locked into his and hardened. "Dad. Can you give us some privacy? I'll call you later."

The General stood up and tucked the paper under his arm. "As I said, I have another appointment. I'll expect to hear from you ASAP, Jesse. I had to call in favors to get you back where you were."

Jesse nodded. "You'll hear from me, sir."

With a deep sigh, the General opened the door. He turned once, surveyed Jesse and Adrienne, sighed again, and quietly departed.

As her father's footsteps faded, Adrienne came to life. "Why are you being so difficult? This is the opportunity of a lifetime."

"For who?"

"For you! I did all this for you." Perfectly timed tears welled up in her beautiful eyes.

"What happens if I don't want to be in the army? What if I want to stay in Denver close to Corrine and Adam?" Had he really said that? "What if I like being a civilian?"

Tears spilled onto her eyelashes, hung for a few moments, then trailed down her flawless skin. "Why are you doing this to me? What about our dream? It was a good dream, wasn't it?"

He was forced to admit she had a point. It *was* a good dream with plenty of rewards along the way. He'd get a new commission, make captain, start climbing the Pentagon ladder again. An honorable life built on solid bedrock, his star rising, his success assured. But he'd changed. In a fundamental way, he'd grown into a man who could never again be the idealistic first lieutenant who left the army with a broken heart and a bleak future.

Gazing into Adrienne Wrightwood's perfect face, he finally accepted that sometime over the past year, he'd fallen out of love with her. He didn't want his old life back. "I'm sorry. This was a mistake."

Her jaw dropped. "I don't believe it. I'm giving you a second chance. Dad went out of his way to help you."

"You should have talked to me before you went ahead. I told you that last night."

Her dark eyes narrowed, and her soft mouth hardened. "My parents, my friends, everyone told me I could do better, but I thought you were special. You told me once that you were going to be a general. I *believed* you."

Lin's voice whispered close to his ear—you always think you're right, and no one could possibly have anything important to teach you. "Someone finally made me see that only idiots believe they control their own future."

He saw the long, lean muscle in her upper arm tighten as she pulled it back. He knew what was coming, but he didn't try to stop her. He deserved this. Her hand cracked across his cheek, knocking his head to the side.

"You bastard!"

His face burned. "I'm sorry. A lot of things happened after I handed in my commission. I've changed, Adrienne. More than I realized. I thought maybe if we spent time together, we could get back the love we had, but it's too late. At least for me."

"Oh, god, there's someone else, isn't there?" Adrienne sank down onto the couch and dropped her face into her hands. He reached out and pressed his palm against her hair. She pushed his arm away. "Leave me alone."

Was there someone else? Did he love Lin?

"Do me one last, little favor," she said.

"Sure. Anything."

"Get out of here so I can pack my bags and leave with what little pride I have left."

His eyes found the armoire. "What about the furniture?"

"Keep it. Just get out."

He picked up his keys and turned back. She was huddled on the sofa, the ultimate picture of misery. By tomorrow, she'd be working the phone, spinning the break-up as her idea and planning her next move. "Thanks."

She lifted her head and gazed at him with teary eyes. Bitterness twisted her face. "For the furniture? For wasting your time? What?"

"For waking me up."

It was time for him to find Linnea and have the talk he'd promised her that last evening in Cloud River when the world was falling to pieces around them. Maybe her life with the senator wasn't working out. Maybe it was his turn to rescue her.

After that? He'd do something wholly out of character for him. Play it by ear.

Chapter Twenty-Eight

Jesse peeled his rented Mustang convertible away from the steamy four-lane highway north of Chicago onto a leafy, tree-lined street. A canopy of oaks and maples shaded the road and a strong easterly breeze cooled his hot face. He breathed in a deep lungful of lake air, leaned back in his seat and took in the sights. Stately mansions peeked out from behind thick hedges and cast iron fences. In the late afternoon heat, gardeners sweated over perfectly manicured lawns. *Lin lived here?*

He double-checked the address on the GPS. It was the one Corrine had given him when she informed him that Lin hadn't married the senator after all. Corrine had also warned him that if he did anything to hurt Linnea, she'd never talk to him again. As if Corrine had the self-control to stop talking. Still, it stung that his mother sided with Lin.

He followed the GPS down a twisting, narrow street, thick with shrubs and sweeping yards of emerald green to a hulking mansion of brown brick with medieval turrets guarding the corners. A high wall surrounded the densely wooded property. Jesse parked near the front door—a heavy, planked affair with wrought-iron hinges that reminded him of a dungeon.

An ordinary girl in a black uniform and white apron answered the door. He'd expected the Bride of Frankenstein.

"May I help you, sir?"

"I'm looking for Linnea Reyes."

The girl frowned. "Linnea's not home."

"When do you expect her back?"

She studied him disapprovingly. "Is she expecting you?"

"Well, no—"

"Who's there?" The female voice sounded like Lin's, only older.

The door swung wide. A thin woman with short gray hair studied him. Wide blue eyes swept boldly down his body, taking in his khaki shorts, polo and topsiders, then back up to his face. "Who are you?"

"Jesse McCormick, ma'am. I came to see Linnea Reyes."

"You must come in and wait." She turned to the maid. "Bring Mr. McCormick a beer. He looks thirsty. I'll have a martini. Don't forget the olive."

He followed his hostess past a set of carved, medieval doors and a wide staircase that rose nearly to the second floor then split in two at a broad landing like an old-time movie set. The lady waved him into a bright sitting room, which seemed to belong to a different house. As he settled into a comfortable chair, an ice-cold micro-brew materialized at his elbow.

His hostess inspected her martini glass and took a sip. "This will do," she said to the maid. "You can leave us. Close the door on your way out."

When the door clicked, the lady turned to Jesse. "I'm Linnea's aunt, Mitchell Basinger. Please call me Mitty."

"Nice to meet you."

"How long have you known my niece?"

"Not long. We met this winter. She came to help my family with some issues we were having. She, uh, decided to work on our organic farm and ended up staying on with us for awhile."

The woman's pale eyebrows popped up. A calculated look flashed crossed her face. "You must be the boyfriend she told me about."

Lin considered him to be her boyfriend? He tried to reconcile that news with the sad girl who said good-by to him last April on her way to becoming engaged to another man. "Maybe."

The old girl seemed to like that answer. She beamed at him. "Tell me about yourself."

"Not much to tell. Spent most of the last dozen years in the army."

"Officer or enlisted?"

"Officer."

"And now?"

"Pilot for a commuter airline."

"College?"

This seemed more like an interview than a conversation. "Yes."

"I meant where and what was your major?"

"West Point. Engineering. Perhaps you'd like to see my résumé."

"Do you have it with you?"

Was she serious? He studied her. She was. "I seem to have missed something here. What is going on?"

She met his eyes straight on without flinching. "I don't have the slightest idea what you're talking about."

He sighed and glanced at his watch. Five thirty. "When does Lin get home?"

The old girl took another sip of her martini. "I insist you stay here at the house while you're in town. We have plenty of room."

Who invited a stranger they'd known for ten minutes to bunk at their house? Had Lin gotten herself tangled up in another sticky situation? "I'm going to ask you one more time, and if I don't get an answer I like, I'm walking out that door. What is going on?"

"Aunt Mitty?" There was a light knock on the door, and Lin's head appeared. "Agatha said you have a visitor—" The blood drained from her face and genuine terror filled her eyes. "Jesse?"

Her face was fuller than he remembered, but her skin glowed with an inner beauty that made his heart beat faster. His body stirred, he itched to touch her, even if it was just a peck on the cheek or a squeeze of her hand. He rose.

"Come on in, dear," said Mitty. "Your friend from Colorado has come for a visit. Isn't that wonderful?"

Lin stepped into the room and leaned on the door until it

closed behind her. She wore a gray pinstripe pantsuit and carried a pair of Adrienne-like high heels in her hands. She stared at him, but seemed incapable of speech.

He met her gaze. "I guess I surprised you."

She nodded.

"Jesse, dear, can you help Linnea to a chair. Poor thing. She's exhausted." His eyes dropped down to Mitty's face. She was studying him—no, assessing him. If General Wrightwood ever set foot in this house, he'd finally meet his match.

He stepped forward cautiously, suddenly not sure if she'd welcome his touch.

The shoes in her hands clattered to the floor. She backed away from him. "I'm fine. No need to help me."

She fumbled behind her back for the door handle. "I better go upstairs. I have some work to finish before tomorrow." She flashed a regretful smile at Jesse. "Sorry we didn't have more time to talk. If you call ahead next time, I'll—"

"Jesse is going to stay with us for a few days. Won't that be nice? You'll have plenty of time to catch up. In fact, on your way upstairs, would you mind telling Agatha to prepare the green guest room and set another place for dinner?"

Lin gave her a shaky nod and slipped out the door.

Chapter Twenty-Nine

Lin sent her regrets at dinner. She was avoiding him, and Jesse was surprised by how much it hurt. Could she have fallen out of love so quickly?

As soon as the plates were cleared, Mitty begged a headache and excused herself. Agatha, the young maid who answered the door earlier, led Jesse up the dramatic staircase and down a dark corridor to the Gothic version of a guest suite—thick curtains of green velvet, murky green walls, heavy mahogany tables, and overstuffed chairs jammed into a small sitting room. Three rusted helmets were mounted on the wall over a stone fireplace. Maybe he'd open the visors later to see if they contained severed heads.

Jesse set down his overnight bag and surveyed the cave-like suite. How had Lin ended up here?

"Is Linnea's room in this wing?"

Agatha nodded. "She sleeps in the tower at the end of the hall. Can I get you anything else before I leave?"

"I'm good. Thanks."

She nodded and closed the door softly behind her.

He counted to fifty, then slipped into the corridor. Oriental runners swept past him and disappeared into gloom. The vaulted ceiling and shadowy walls pressed in on him. Dimly lit, wrought-iron chandeliers circled above him like vultures. A suit of armor stood at attention with a rusty hatchet clasped in its empty glove, the sightless eyeholes evoking visions of torture chambers and dungeons. Wariness crept through him as he headed into the shadows.

Beneath the tower door, a pale band of light glimmered. He scanned the corridor, eyes straining into the darkness. The silence was absolute. A door opened and closed in Lin's room, but out in the medieval darkness, nothing stirred. Damn the consequences, he was going in.

He pushed the door open a crack and slipped inside. Perimeter breached.

The gothic world stopped at the threshold to Lin's room. Creamy walls and pale carpeting glowed in soft light from a bedside table. A bed with a simple white headboard was turned down for the night. At high, arched windows, a hearty breeze blew at thin curtains. Beneath them, an open book rested face down on a bench scattered with throw pillows.

He closed his eyes and breathed deeply. The scent of Lin's herbal shampoo filled his nostrils and brought back pleasant memories of holding her naked body in his arms.

On the far side of the room, a door swung open. Lin wandered out of her bathroom, towel-drying her damp hair. A virginal white cotton nightgown covered her slender body. It was sheer enough for a shadowy glimpse of her nipples and a pair of pink panties, probably cotton, too. The folds of the gown fell modestly to her ankles with a girlish ruffle. His body stirred as he stepped into the light.

The towel slipped from her hands. "What are you doing in my room?"

He held up his hands. "I just came to talk."

She snatched up her towel and used it to shield her body from him. "You could have warned me. I'm not dressed."

"Come on, Lin. You're wearing more clothes than most teenagers. Besides," he arched a brow, "I've seen your body before."

"It was a mistake."

She wasn't going to make this easy for him. He cleared his throat and prepared to grovel. "It wasn't a mistake."

"I'll bet your girlfriend wouldn't agree."

Of course. Corrine would have told Lin about Adrienne. "*That* was a mistake."

"Whatever. You don't owe me anything so there's no reason for you to stick around."

"Owe you?"

She blushed. "I mean about the money. Aunt Mitty didn't break a sweat when she signed the check."

"For chrissake, Lin. Didn't Corrine tell you?"

"Tell me what?"

"You didn't have to marry the senator."

She shifted her weight. "I don't understand."

"I figured out what the Coopers were after. It was the statues. They're worth a lot of money. I came after you when we found out what you did, but you were already gone." He tilted his head and studied her.

"Either way, I had to go. You know that."

He'd been such a jerk the last day. "Can we talk about what happened? That's why I came here."

Wary eyes watched him, tightly fisted hands inched the towel closer to her neck. "I still want Corrine to have the money. So if that's what you're here about, you can leave with a clear conscience."

"I came to see you."

"Well, you've seen me. Obviously I am doing great."

"I don't believe you," he said.

"I know I said some things about love this spring that were a little out there, but I've recovered my sanity, if that's what you're here about." A strained smile puckered her lips. She made a small bow. "Go back to your room and pack your bags with a clear conscience."

She sure was anxious to get rid of him. Why? "Can we talk for a few minutes? Please, Lin. I've come all this way just to see you."

Her body swayed as a stiff breeze swirled through the turret, but her expression softened, and the old Lin appeared. "Just for a few minutes." She nodded toward the window seat. "Do you want to sit down?"

She settled on the bench, pulling her nightgown over her knees and drawing them to her chest before dropping the towel to the floor. A warm breeze caught up the thin cotton like a sail making it billow around her.

"Look, Jess, I am happy for you and Corrine, and Adam, too. You guys deserve some happiness. And it's so nice of you to come see me. But our lives have changed. I'm with Aunt Mitty now, and you have all those adventures to chase after."

"That's a very nice speech, and I don't believe a word of it. You seem hell-bent on getting me out of Frankenstein's dungeon. Why?"

The old, sweet Lin vanished, replaced by the jittery, slightly terrified modern version. She sniffed at him. "That's ridiculous. I think I was very clear when I left that I didn't want to see you, and I'm sure you have more interesting things to do than fly halfway across the country to visit me."

She took a deep cleansing breath, then another, and pursed her lips as she studied him. "Honest, Jesse, I'm fine." Her gray eyes pleaded with him. "Go back to Colorado. Fly your beloved airplanes. Travel the world."

He knew that look. "You are not telling the truth."

"I am." Her arms tightened around her knees.

She was being stubborn, but he'd sweet-talked the truth out of her before. "Look, baby." He wanted to press his hand to her leg, but he wasn't sure she'd welcome his touch. He gentled his voice instead. "I'll make a deal with you. Tell me to go and I'll leave first thing in the morning. If that's what you really want." Operative word—*really*.

"Go."

"Look me in the eye and say that."

Thunder rumbled in the distance. A sudden gust of grass-scented wind push the curtains high into the air. As they drifted down from the ceiling, a panel landed on Lin's head and twisted around her shoulders. She slid off the window seat and lifted her arms to untangle it.

The gold light from the bedside table pierced her thin nightgown, limning her body with light. His eyes traced the curve of her breasts and followed the outline of her body to her waist. He froze.

Everything Mitty and Lin had said—and done—since he stepped into this house suddenly made sense.

*

Jesse's hand jerked the hem of her nightgown up to her ribs. Linnea squealed and pushed away from him. But his free hand slid over her upper arm, stopping her before she could move.

"How dare you!" She tugged at her gown. It didn't budge.

"I could say the same thing to you."

She yanked on the hem of her nightgown, tearing it. Why did he always have to react so physically? "I mean it, Jesse. Let me go, or …"

"Or what? You'll scream? You'll wake up the entire house so we can have it out in front of Mitty and the maids?" His furious words careened off the walls, the ceiling and the floor of her little tower.

"Have what out? What are you talking about? Why are you mauling me?" *He knows.*

"You're pregnant."

It was already a lost battle, but she tried one last time to fend him off. "Pregnant? You must be suffering from post-traumatic stress disorder." She tried to pull away.

"That is low." He tugged her back to him by the handful of cotton nightie he held tight in his fist.

"Really? First you sneak into my bedroom uninvited and now you're seeing babies popping up in tummies. I've gained a little weight since I came to Chicago."

"Bullshit."

"Honest, Jesse. That's all it is."

"I'll bet your aunt has a different story."

A deep weariness overcame Linnea. The whole world was against her—even her goldfish who'd only lived two days. The curtain billowed against her head again, and she batted it away angrily.

"Okay, I'm pregnant. It probably happened at the lodge. In the shower."

She smoothed down her wrinkly nightgown and recited the story she told herself whenever she got a case of the guilts. "But I can take care of it myself. I have plenty of money and Aunt Mitty is going to help me. I don't need you. The baby doesn't need you."

She'd give her baby everything her mother hadn't been able to give her. Except a father. She'd always promised herself that her children would know their father.

"That's not your decision to make without me."

A streak of lightning shot across the sky followed by a loud crack of thunder. Rain blew through the screen. The cold water felt good against her skin. Jesse reached over her and shut the window. As he straightened, his hand brushed at the drops of rain spattered across her arm. Warmth flooded her body. It was time to face the truth. She loved him. Maybe more than ever.

He sat down beside her and gripped his knees. His hands were smooth, his nails clean. The real Jesse. The man meant for big things, not the down-on-his-luck farmer who'd taken a passing interest in her.

"Did you know about the baby when you left Cloud River?" he asked.

For the first time ever she'd been late, and the knowledge had filled her with a joy so strong it took her breath away. "I suspected."

"You didn't think it was your duty to inform me?"

"Look, Jess, you told me you didn't want to be tied down. Just friends. Remember?"

"And you said you were taking a job in Greeley."

"Did not. You assumed that I was going to Greeley. Which is typical of you."

"What the hell is *that* supposed to mean?"

"It means that you expect everyone around you to be obedient little soldiers and do exactly what you expect of them."

Another bolt of lightning lit up the sky, reflecting the planes of Jesse's face and the sharp downturn of his mouth. "Well, that doesn't seem to be working very well for me, does it?"

"I guess not."

"Besides, this has nothing to do with what I expect. This is about what is right."

His strong sense of right and wrong was one of the things she loved best about him. That and his smile and the way he called her "baby" and how his mere presence could light up her day. She gazed around her cozy tower room. "What do you want?"

Her hand was engulfed in a strong, masculine grip, and her body began to melt. *Careful, girl.* Against her will, her eyes raised to meet his. The gold in his irises glittered like a thousand stars. "I came here because I've been thinking about you lately. I wanted to see if there was anything between us."

"I see."

"All that's changed. I, uh, we have a child on the way. A child that is as much my responsibility as yours."

"I told you, I can take care of it myself."

"That's not the point."

He wanted something from her, and she was not going to like it. "What is the point, Jesse? It's getting late." She pulled her hands from him and buried them in her lap.

"I want to marry you."

She jumped from the window seat. "Marry! Are you out of your freaking mind?"

He grabbed her arm and pulled her down beside him again.

"We care about each other, Lin, and we'd make good parents. I can't walk away from you and the baby. If you understand anything about me, you know this."

Why couldn't she hate him? Better yet, why couldn't he love her?

"It's the twenty-first century, Jess. People don't marry just because someone gets pregnant. There are a million perfectly happy single moms and dads out there with well-adjusted kids."

He leaned into her. His face hovered over hers, his mouth centimeters from hers. His skin smelled spicy and a little sweaty and masculine. "I wouldn't ask if I didn't care about you, Lin. I want us to be a tight circle like Robbie and Corrine were with Adam and me." He kissed her softly.

She pushed him away. "Stop kissing me."

He leaned back. "Well?"

"Robbie and Corrine loved each other. You're proposing a legal charade to satisfy your sense of duty."

He had the grace to bow his head. "I don't know how I feel, Lin. But I promise to give you and the baby the best of me. Please, Lin. Don't shut me out."

A wave of love and protectiveness poured over her. *Damn him for saying just the right thing at the wrong time.* Maybe she had enough love for both of them until he learned to love her. After the baby came, she'd take flying lessons. Jump out of airplanes with a parachute on her back. Climb mountains. Whatever. They'd have adventures together. She'd be everything he'd ever wanted in a wife.

"Maybe it would work," she said.

"Let's do it right away. Tomorrow."

He wanted to get married tomorrow? What about Aunt Mitty and Basinger Industries? "It's too soon. I need a little time to adjust."

His eyes swept down her translucent nightgown, warming her skin as his gaze passed over her. "Are you sure?"

She smiled despite herself. "Stop trying to seduce me."

"Impossible." Pulling her hard against him, he kissed her until her lips burned. Then he drew back. "I want to marry you now." When she started to protest, he added, "You've already snuck out on me once."

But what if he changed his mind once they got back to Colorado? Or ran into Adrienne again or Ashley? "You have to give me some time to think about it." Did she dare risk her heart on him again?

"How many hours?" He grinned.

"I mean it. The baby isn't due until December. Go home. I'll let you know in a few weeks."

Chapter Thirty

Someone was knocking softly on his bedroom door. "Mr. McCormick?"

Jesse rolled out of bed and felt his way through the dark sitting room. It was Agatha. He tightened the string on his sweatpants. "What?"

"It's Linnea." He pushed past Agatha and ran toward the tower. The door was wide open, and Linnea's bed was empty.

His gut twisted with fear. "Where is she?"

Agatha sniffed. "She lost the baby. Miss Basinger took her to the hospital an hour ago."

"Why didn't you wake me."

Tears were running down Agatha's face. "She said not to disturb you, but Ms. Basinger just called. She said to tell you."

The next thirty minutes were a blur. One moment he was jerking on his pants, and the next, he was running through the main entrance of the hospital. There was the face of an elderly nurse pointing the way to Lin's room, but he didn't remember any words. When he burst into Lin's room, Mitty stood up. "I'll leave you two alone."

Lin lay curled in a ball on the hospital bed. He dropped to his knees so he could look into her face. She was crying. He brushed her hair back from her face.

"You didn't have to come, Jesse. I feel so stupid."

"It's not your fault."

"I wanted a baby so bad, and I never thought I'd have one."

His heart hurt. "You'll have more."

She shook her head sadly. "What if I don't?"

He didn't know what to say so he kissed her cheek. "Just get better. Okay?"

"Don't leave me."

"I won't."

He kicked off his shoes and lay down in the bed with Lin, pulling her back against his chest, cupping her body with his own. Her hair still smelled of shampoo and the scent of sleep clung to her skin. She wept softly and inside, he wept with her. He kissed the top of her head.

"I was happy about the baby, too."

"Really?"

"Yeah, really."

"I always screw things up, don't I?"

"No." He pressed his hands to her ribs so he could feel her heart beat. "It's good to hold you again."

Her sniffling stopped. "Honest?"

He nuzzled her hair. "Yeah." His eyes stung. He never wanted to let her go.

"I'm tired." She snuggled closer.

"Close your eyes. Rest."

"Will you stay with me?"

"I will." *Forever, if you let me.*

*

"It's such a beautiful night. Thanks for dragging me out to dinner." Lin's lips curled into a sad smile.

Jesse's heart clutch "I'm glad Mitty's a little better."

"Dragging" barely put a dent in the list of what he had to do to get her out of Mitty's hospital room. Two days after Lin's miscarriage, Mitty had a mild heart attack, which was blamed on her chemo drugs. Since Lin had climbed into the ambulance with Mitty nearly a week ago, he'd barely seen her, and he'd finally been forced to breach hospital security to beg for one evening alone with her.

She'd agreed to dinner, but only after Mitty fell asleep. Somewhere between Mitty's room and the main hospital entrance where he picked her up, she'd put on a yellow dress with thin straps and matching sandals. Long crystal earrings tangled with her hair, which she'd left free—the way he loved it most.

"Don't you like your pasta?" he asked. She'd barely touched her food.

"I love it. Honest." An earring caught the reflection of the twinkling Italian lights strung across the outdoor patio and sparkled against her jaw.

"Then why aren't you eating?"

"I'm too knotted up inside." Her eyes shimmered.

"Did you see the full moon tonight?" he asked in a gentle, soothing voice.

"No." She tilted her face toward the sky.

"Other way."

She turned. "It's so bright. I love it."

He followed her gaze. "Corrine knows the name of every full moon."

"They have names?"

"Well, there's the Harvest Moon. Everyone's heard of that. But in July, it's the Full Buck Moon."

"Sounds dirty." She giggled, reminding him of the nights he listened to her muffled laughter through Corrine's bedroom door. It seemed like a thousand years ago.

He grinned. "Get your mind out of the gutter. It's called that because stags begin to grow their new antlers in July."

Her cheeks turned pink, and he reached across the table and squeezed her hand. "You look great tonight. This is the first time I've seen you dressed up."

Beside her plate, a small silk evening purse began to vibrate. Lin pulled her hand away. "It must be Aunt Mitty."

He swallowed his frustration as he leaned back.

"Yes? Aunt Mitty?" Lin listened for a moment. "I'm with Jesse. We're just ten minutes from the hospital." Another pause. "I'll be there as soon as I can."

She slid the phone back into her purse. "I'm sorry. Aunt Mitty woke up. She's asking for me. I've got to go."

He tried to relax as he signaled the waiter for the check but his foot wouldn't stop tapping on the flagstones. Tense silence stretched between them on the drive back to the hospital.

He felt her studying him. "What?" he asked.

"Why are you still here?"

Why indeed? He'd asked himself that same question, and the answer had risen up in him like a bright bubble of joy. He'd fallen in love with Lin. Hell, maybe he'd always loved her and been too stubborn to admit it.

He pulled into a parking space near the hospital's main entrance. "Come on. Let's walk for a few minutes."

"Jesse—"

"Mitty is in good hands. We need to talk."

They crossed the parking lot to a grassy lawn with a narrow walking path curling along the edge. She stooped and pulled off her sandals. Then she started to walk again, swinging a shoe in each hand.

"I don't think there's anything more to say, Jess. I belong here with my aunt. You have a life of adventure waiting out there for you."

"No."

He was working up his nerve to say more when her cell phone vibrated again. She dropped her sandals on the sidewalk and opened her purse. He snatched the phone from her hand and growled into the receiver. "She'll be there when we're done talking." Then he turned off the phone and handed it back. "Here."

"How could you? Aunt Mitty is—"

He'd reached the end of his patience. "Aunt Mitty is in a great hospital attended by a battalion of the best doctors and nurses money can buy. She'll manage without you for one evening."

Tears glistened in Lin's eyes.

He felt like a shit. "Sorry. I guess I just don't understand."

"She needs me."

"Stop it, Lin! You don't have to ride to the rescue every time someone gets a fricking paper cut."

Lin's mouth tightened. "Aunt Mitty does not have a paper cut, and you know it."

"Why do you always put everyone before yourself? Running off to marry some pervert to make Corrine happy. Barricading yourself in that creepy mansion to make your aunt happy. Spending day after day in the hospital. Look how thin you've gotten. You're not taking care of yourself."

Her eyes flashed angrily, reminding him of the old Lin, and she came right back at him. "You quit your army career to help your family."

"That's different."

"Why, Jesse. Explain to me why you can sacrifice and be noble, and I can't."

"Because I know how to handle tough situations without going overboard."

"Joining an army of mercenaries and flying off to Colombia isn't 'going overboard'?"

"I had the situation under control." *Like hell.*

"Don't you dare pretend you knew what you were doing." She spun away from him and began to walk. "You are the most ungrateful man I've ever met."

"Hold on!" How had this gotten so turned around?

"I've got to get back."

He slid a hand around her wrist and felt an instant surge of desire as her soft skin warmed his palm. "Please. I'm sorry."

She stopped.

"I didn't bring you here to fight. I want to talk to you." He examined the thin wrist wrapped in his fingers while he grasped for a thread from the tight ball of emotions inside him.

"I proposed to you."

She pulled her hand away. "That was before the miscarriage. Consider yourself absolved of your obligation."

"That's not what I meant."

"Come on, Jesse. You never wanted to be married, and I am a miserable failure at everything I do, especially relationships." She swiped a tear from her cheek. "I can't believe I was going to take up skydiving just to make you happy."

"For chrissake, Lin. You make me happy just the way you are. Why would I want you to risk your life jumping out of planes?"

"That's what I mean. I'm a failure. Besides, someone has to run Basinger."

"You shouldn't be locked up in an office building. You'll wither and die."

"Aunt Mitty says I'll ease into the job. I just need more time." She glanced impatiently up at the lighted hospital windows. "I have to run."

"Lin, wait." He gazed into her eyes but saw no encouragement. He took the plunge anyway. What else could he do? "I know it's taken me four months to say it back, but I love you."

Her eyes grew dark and bottomless. "Why do you have to do this now?"

He didn't know what to say.

"I can't be with you. Don't you understand?" Tears spilled out of her eyes. She rubbed them away impatiently. "All I do is cry."

He took a step closer. "Lin. Baby."

She held her hand out and stopped his advance. "No. Don't touch me. I'm sorry, Jesse. But I just don't have anything left inside for you." She waved her hand in the direction of the hospital. "Aunt Mitty needs me."

His mouth was stiff, and he had to push out the words. "Sorry to have bothered you. I'll get out of your way."

Her face crumpled. "Where are you going?"

Why did she care? "Home."

She flinched.

"It was your home, too."

Tear began to stream down her cheeks, and this time she didn't try to brush them away.

He tried one last time. "It could be again. Corrine and Adam miss you. I miss you."

"I can't." Then she pushed past him and ran barefoot down the path, a yellow flame that burned the man who dared to come too close.

Chapter Thirty-One

From the lumpy cot next to Aunt Mitty's bed, Linnea watched the pale fingers of the morning sun poke away the night. A squeaky-footed nurse hurried past the door, then an elevator dinged in the distance and a heavy set of wheels clattered over the threshold. Mornings began early in the hospital.

Her body felt heavy with exhaustion. Too heavy to lift off the cot. So she studied the trees swaying in the morning breeze and let the images of last night come to her. Where was Jesse right now? What was he feeling? Would he ever forgive her?

Rejecting him had hurt, but beneath the hurt irritation festered. Why did he wait so long to fall in love? Didn't he understand it was too late for them? Her passion had bled away with the baby, and Aunt Mitty and the company sucked up what few drops of vitality were left. There was nothing inside her, even for him.

Her phone vibrated, and she pulled it from beneath her pillow. Corrine. What had Jesse told her? In her drug-induced sleep, Aunt Mitty groaned and her eyelids fluttered. The phone vibrated again.

"Hello?" Linnea spoke softly as she tiptoed out into the hall.

"It's Corrine."

"I know."

"Jesse came home about an hour ago." There was a long pause. "He woke me up and told me what happened."

She stared down at her feet as two orderlies passed with a gurney. Why couldn't people just leave her alone? "I'm not sure what you're talking about."

"Everything. I wish you'd told me."

Hot tears filled Linnea's eyes. "You're mad."

Corrine sighed. "I'm so sorry about the baby. You must be very sad."

Linnea leaned against the wall and closed her eyes. Exhaustion weighed on her like a lead coat. She could barely stand. "I'll be okay." The words slurred together.

"Oh, Linnea, I wish I could be there with you. I know what you're going through." Corrine spoke the words softly.

A spark of indignation ignited inside her. No one knew what she felt. Then it died. She didn't have the energy to fight.

"Before I had Jesse, I lost a baby, too."

Linnea watched a mother and two teenage daughters come down the corridor, swinging their heads from side-to-side as they read the numbers on the doors, unaware of her loss. She waited until they passed. "I didn't know."

"I don't talk about it much. It still hurts a little."

"It never goes away?" She couldn't live like this forever.

"It gets better. I promise. After my miscarriage I stopped caring about myself. I lay on the couch all day. I couldn't even find the strength to shower or eat. Robbie was so patient. He'd work all day, then come and sit beside my smelly self and listen as I talked the worst of the horrible ache out of me. I was so afraid I'd never have a baby. Robbie would say, 'I'll love you no matter what.'"

"I don't have anyone to talk to."

"What about Jesse? He loves you."

"I can't. We didn't start out like you and Robbie."

"I know. Still, if you ever need a sympathetic ear, he'll be there for you. So will I. No matter what happens with Jesse."

Something inside Linnea loosened.

"We are family, Linnea. You can always talk to me."

Chapter Thirty-Two

From Aunt Mitty's hospital room, Linnea stared out at a moonless night. The dark sky matched her gloomy mood. What would become of her?

Behind her, Aunt Mitty cleared her throat, Linnea turned away from the window. "How are you feeling?"

"Much better than a few weeks ago." Clear blue eyes, sparkling with intelligence, studied Linnea. How long had she been awake? Had she sensed Linnea's unhappiness?

"I'm glad you're going to be okay, Aunt Mitty." Although a half-dozen wires and tubes still snaked from her aunt's thin body, she'd made a remarkable recovery. The doctors had agreed to discharge her in two days.

Aunt Mitty cleared her throat. "You look so sad lately."

"I'm fine. It's just the baby and … things."

Aunt Mitty extended a thin arm toward Linnea. "Come here." Abandoning her perch on the window sill, Linnea slipped her hand into Aunt Mitty's cool grasp. "You've been so good to me, my dear."

Linnea frowned. "Aunt Mitty—"

"Let me have my say. When I first came for you, my thoughts were on Basinger and my need for an heir. But your loyalty and patience with an old lady has touched me deeply. So it breaks my heart to see you so sad."

What was the point of burdening Aunt Mitty with her problems? "I'm not sad. Just a little tired, maybe."

"I know sad when I see it." The thin hand squeezed Linnea's. "Come and sit. Tell me what's bothering you."

"I can't." Aunt Mitty would think it was her fault that Jesse was gone.

"It's Jesse, isn't it? You miss him."

Linnea's heart contracted, and tears sprang to her eyes. She sank down the bed. "I was so horrible to him. He said he loved me, and I hurt him. He probably hates me."

"Did his mother tell you that?"

Linnea brushed the tears from her cheeks but more took their place. "I never called her back after that day. She must hate me, too. For hurting Jesse."

"Do you love Jesse? Is that why you're unhappy?"

"It doesn't matter. I'm here with you now. As soon as you're settled at home, I'll go back to work at Basinger."

Aunt Mitty's eyes were wise as she patted Linnea's hand. "I love you, my dear. Very much. But I've come to the conclusion that you're not cut out for the corporate life."

She'd sacrificed Jesse to help with Basinger. If Aunt Mitty took that away, she'd truly have nothing left. "I just need more time. Please."

"I have no doubt you will eventually learn to read a financial statement and run a board meeting. But I doubt these things will ever make you happy, and I want you to be happy."

This wasn't making sense. Was Aunt Mitty going to hand Basinger over to Julian? "But what about Basinger? I'm the only one who can help you."

"The rule is a family member. That would include an in-law like a husband, if you found one who was qualified, and I believe Jesse would do nicely."

"What if he won't forgive me?" A vision of Ashley Cooper flashed through her head. "Or what if he's moved on?"

"Nonsense. It's only been a few weeks. A heartbroken man doesn't recover that quickly." Aunt Mitty smiled up at her. "You have a generous spirit, my dear, but so do other people. Give the rest of us a chance to be generous to you. You deserve it."

The thick emotions blanketing Linnea thinned and dissolved. Jesse had sworn his love. He wouldn't have moved on already. Would he? It was time to find out if he'd meant what he said ... and if she had the courage to ask.

Chapter Thirty-Three

For sentimental reasons, she requested a Silverado at the Denver airport, but the man at the rental counter didn't have one in the lot. Linnea took a Chevy Tahoe instead because it was big and white. As she spun off the exit to Cloud River she got the jitters. She'd wanted to surprise Jesse, but maybe that was a mistake.

She steered the truck onto Canyon Road, remembering the first time she'd come here. In the mid-summer evening, the houses seemed happier than they had in early March, and when she topped the rise, no smoke curled from the chimney of the turquoise house. But lights twinkled in the windows.

Knocking on the door, she waited with a pounding heart and dry throat, adjusting her blue silk dress, wishing she'd dressed more casually. She'd tried to steel herself for rejection, but if the McCormicks were through with her, no amount of preparation could spare her pain.

The door swung open. Corrine stood in the glow of the living room lamps. When she saw Linnea her face lit up and she squealed. "Linnea! You've come home!" She pulled Linnea into her arms and squeezed. Linnea hugged her back as relief and gratitude warmed her shaky body.

"Is Jesse here?"

Corrine smiled. "I told him to be patient."

Did he listen?

"Actually you just missed him. It's Teddy's birthday, and they're celebrating at the brewery." Corrine stood back from the door. "I'm meeting Harry for dinner, but you can come in and wait."

If she had to wait alone in this house all night to discover her fate, she'd lose her nerve. Besides, if Jesse didn't want her, retreat would be easier on neutral ground. "Do you think it would be okay if I went to the brewery?"

*

Linnea rumbled into Cloud River, tooting her horn as she passed the old supermarket, and hung a right on First Street. The little shops were closed, but the parking lot at the brewery was full and voices raised in laughter and celebration floated out into the deepening night.

Inside the brewery, knots of people hugged the bar, mugs of beer clasped tight in their hands. A man—was it Teddy?—turned his head and saw her. She watched his eyes widen before he turned away. A moment later, Jesse detached himself from Teddy's cluster.

He strode toward her, tall and handsome in a black shirt and jeans. His face was unreadable, and she didn't know if she'd done the right thing.

"Why did you come?" His eyes glittered with wariness.

She couldn't breathe.

"I'd nearly given up. I figured you couldn't forgive me for trying to push myself on you."

"No, Jesse." She touched his arm. It was warm and solid. Desire flowered inside her. "I was never mad at you."

"But—"

"I was in hormonal hell. It made me a little crazy for awhile."

"That's what Corrine said."

"And I missed the baby." She hesitated before plunging ahead. If their future was going to have a chance, she had to be open with him. "What if I can't get pregnant again?"

"We'll cross that bridge when we come to it." He hesitated. "Together, if you'll have me."

"Jesse." Her throat contracted around his name.

He took her hands in his, brushing her fingers with his thumb, warming her skin. "I want forever with you."

"Are you proposing?"

He glanced over his shoulder. She followed his gaze. Teddy and a flock of Jesse's friends watched them with open curiosity. "Hell," he muttered, then dropped to one knee in the middle of the bar. Slowly, one-by-one, the laughter and chatter died away. Jesse tipped his head up and captured his gaze. The gold in his eyes shimmered with emotion. "I love you, Lin, more than I've ever loved anyone. You taught me that sometimes just being true to yourself can beat all the strategy in the world. You also taught me that not just soldiers have honor and courage. Crazy, beautiful girls with blond ponytails have it, too."

Winning and losing, soldiers and courage. That was her Jesse. She loved him so much.

"Linnea, will you do me the honor of becoming my wife."

She wanted to sink down to the floor with him—and if they'd been alone, she would have. But instead she smiled into his eyes. "Yes. Yes, I will."

He rose and scooped her into his arms and gave her a soft, sweet kiss. Behind him, applause and cheers erupted, but she barely noticed.

*

The turquoise house shimmered like a deep pool in the moonlight. Jesse pushed open the front door and scooped her into his arms, carrying her through the kitchen and into his bedroom.

He bent his head and kissed her before setting her down. "I'm sorry."

She brushed a knuckle across his cheekbone. "Sorry for what?"

"This isn't very romantic. You deserve Paris or New York."

"I love you so much." She nuzzled his neck and kissed the pulse point beneath his ear lobe. "Tonight I don't want romantic." She unbuttoned his shirt slowly, pulling it open, and slid her hands up the hard planes of his chest. Her belly tightened.

"What then?" His voice was husky.

She kissed his pecs. "I want sexy."

"Undo your hair."

She lifted her arms to her ponytail.

He shook his head. "Wait. Not yet." Then he spun her around. Cool air hit her spine as he slid down the zipper on her dress. His hands pushed the dress off her shoulders and it slipped down her body to puddle at her feet. She wore nothing but a lacy blue bra and matching panties. A warm mouth nuzzled the back of her neck. Deft finger worked the bra clasp. "I like your underwear." Her bra slipped to the floor. His mouth pressed kisses down her spine to her waist. He slid his hands inside the waistband of her panties and pushed them to her ankles.

He stepped back from her. "Now."

She turned and stretched her arms languidly up to her neck while his eyes roamed her naked body. Slowly she loosened her hair until it fell free around her shoulders.

"You are so beautiful, baby."

She smiled. Her hands went for his belt. "Do you need some help?"

He gazed down into her face and entwined her hair in his fingers. "Maybe." He kissed her, his mouth devouring her lips, his tongue twisting with hers.

She fumbled for his belt, her body already wet, her desire for him a throbbing need. His hardness pressed against her belly, and she pushed down his zipper. She was ready. He stepped back from her. "I want you. Please, Jess."

His generous mouth curved into a smile. Still half-dressed, he laid her onto the bed and knelt between her thighs. He bent and kissed each thigh. Her desire tightened. She was slipping. "No, Jesse. Together. Clothes off. Face to face." The words came out as little gasps.

He lifted his head. "You said sexy."

They could argue the point later. She needed him now. "Romantic."

He shrugged out of his shirt and pushed off his pants and boxers. Then his body moved over her, naked, hard, glistening, perfect. She felt his sweet weight settle on her and raised her hips to him. His mouth sought and found hers, and their tongues intertwined. His penis pressed against her, seeking entrance. Her hand reached between them and guided him. With a groan of pleasure, he thrust into her, stretching her body to fit him. He thrust again, harder, filling her completely.

He pulled his mouth away and nibbled her ear. "Wrap your legs around me, baby."

She did. Clinging to her love, she raised her hips to meet his plunges until her body released and spun, and with a cry of pleasure, Jesse's did too. For a long time she held him against her, stroking his shoulders as the crickets sang softly outside the window.

Finally Jesse stirred. He slipped off her and pulled her against him, spooning her body in his. His mouth moved in her hair. "Well, where do we go from here?"

She braced herself. "We get married and enjoy ourselves for a few weeks."

"And then?"

"You have an appointment with Aunt Mitty two weeks from Monday to take my place running Basinger Industries. Nine a.m. Welcome to the family."

She waited for the explosion, but it didn't come. "We'll get our own place in Chicago. I am not living in that medieval mess your aunt calls home."

"What about Cloud River? Your family is here."

"I haven't belonged here since I was eighteen. There's nothing for me to do here. I need more than a tea garden to be happy."

She giggled and rolled over the face him. "We complement each other perfectly."

His eyes deepened to pools of forest green. "In more ways than one. Come here."

About Mari Manning

Mari Manning lives in the Chicago suburbs with her husband and has two grown daughters. *Angel Without Wings* is her second novel. She is also the author of *Holding Out for a Hero*, which was published by Crimson Press in June 2012. She is working on her third and fourth books. You can contact Mari by visiting her website: *www.marimanning.com*.

More From This Author

Holding Out for a Hero by Mari Manning

*http://www.crimsonromance.com/crimson-romance-ebooks/
crimson-romance-book-genres/romance-suspense-novels/
holding-out-for-a-hero/]*

Chapter 1

Seneca Simms hurried down the narrow corridor, scanning the numbers on the office doors as she brushed past them. When she reached number 425, she stopped. Through frosted glass and thick black letters announcing *Collin Atlee, Private Investigator,* she saw the shadowy figure of a man hunkered over a computer.

"Gotcha."

She twisted the knob and pushed. For a moment the door stuck in the frame. Then it gave, banging against the wall with a dull thud, and Seneca gazed at the most beautiful man she'd ever seen. His features were sharply cut, forehead high, cheekbones prominent, nose straight. His mouth was generous, almost sensual, a feature the dark stubble covering his square jaw failed to hide. Beneath blond hair and dark brows, long-lashed eyes glittered like a king's ransom of sapphires.

A few seconds ticked by while Seneca adjusted to the presence of a handsome stranger sitting in Collin Atlee's office. He frowned at her, perfect brows knitting over the sharp bridge of his nose. Concern creased the corners of his mouth.

Seneca hitched up the heavy purse slung over her shoulder and folded her arms. "Where is Collin Atlee?"

Mr. Beautiful's eyes narrowed until the blue barely showed beneath his sweep of lashes. "If you are looking for Richard, ma'am, you're on the wrong side of town."

"I'm looking for the guy whose name is on the door." She jerked her head sideways at the lettered glass. "Collin Atlee."

His head tipped back. His eyes widened in surprise. "I'm Collin Atlee."

"I've met Mr. Atlee, and you are not him. If you don't tell me where he is right now, I'll-I'll . . ." What would she do? She itched to punch him, but from the width of his shoulders, she guessed a jab delivered by a woman barely five-foot-two wouldn't convince him to start talking.

"Who are you?" he asked.

"You know very well who I am. Mr. Atlee put you up to this, didn't he?"

Mr. Beautiful rose to an intimidating height, requiring her to tilt her head to keep an eye on him. As he came around the desk, he fished something out of the back pocket of his desert camo combat pants. He produced a worn leather wallet and flipped it open. An Illinois state driver's license with the name *Collin R. Atlee* stared out at her along with a fairly hot DMV photo.

She gaped at the picture. Red hot anger exploded behind her eyes.

"Are you all right?"

"How could I be all right? A bumbling, addle-brained *jerk* screwed with me. I've been on pins and needles for a month, waiting for his report—"

"Report? What report? Who *are* you? What are you talking about?"

Poppy's voice spoke in her head. *Breathe deep, Sen. Take it one step at a time.* She took a cleansing breath, then tipped up her chin and eyed the genuine Collin Atlee. "I better go. Obviously there was a mix-up of some kind. You are not the man I talked to last month." If she wanted to resolve her problem in two weeks—and what choice did she have—she'd better get cracking.

He slid his wallet back into his pants. "You talked to someone last month who said he was me?"

"Yes."

"In this office. With my name on the door."

"Yes. Just after Labor Day."

"You're sure."

"Of course I'm sure." She stepped back. "I've got to go."

"What did he look like?"

She let her eyes drift down his body, taking in the black T-shirt, the camo pants, the long legs. "The opposite of you. Short for a man, sort of light brown hair, brown eyes, and well-dressed."

One perfect eyebrow lifted.

"He asked me a lot of questions, mostly about myself, but he didn't write anything down except for my phone number."

"I'll bet." He muttered the words under his breath.

"What's that supposed to mean?"

He gestured toward the set of chairs in front of his desk. "I'm sorry for any trouble this guy caused you. I'd like to make it up."

Chicago is a big city, Sen. You can't trust people. She studied his desk. It was cheap and battered, but his laptop looked new. He kept no photos or other personal items on the desk. A Styrofoam cup held a motley assortment of pens and pencils, an iPhone glowed beside the laptop and a white paper bag with the Golden Arches printed on the front teetered atop a stack of unopened mail. In the window, behind a comfortable leather chair, an ancient air conditioner rattled. Spartan, definitely masculine, but it said nothing about the man himself.

"I don't know."

"Do you need help or don't you? From the way you burst into my office I thought you came about an urgent matter."

An urgent matter that should have been resolved by now. Her fists bunched at her side as her temper inched up toward the danger level again. Maybe he noticed because he backed away from her.

"I'll get you some water." He strode around his desk, back ramrod straight, shoulders thrown back, a posture Seneca had seen hundreds of times. Half the boys in her little hometown joined the military after high school, and when they came back they walked just like Collin Atlee.

Relief washed over her. "You're a soldier, Mr. Atlee."

He dug around in a canvas bag dangling from a bent coat rack and pulled out a bottle of water. "Yup. Call me Collin."

"Seneca Simms."

He twisted the cap off the bottle. His long arm, tattooed just above his elbow with a combat knife and crossed arrows, reached over the desk. Familiar ink on the streets of her hometown. He handed the water to her. "Have a seat."

She lowered herself into one of the visitors' chairs. "I don't know where to start exactly."

"The beginning."

She frowned. "That's my problem. I don't know how to find the beginning."

Tiny smile lines creased the corners of his mouth. "Just dive in. We'll straighten the chronology out later."

She nodded and looked down at her hands. "Well, my father, his name was Woodrow Simms, died last May."

"In Chicago?"

"No. Peabody, West Virginia. I was born, uh, raised there. Anyway, I drove down to Peabody over the Labor Day weekend to sort through his papers and clean out the house. I discovered a birth certificate for a Seneca Albers Simms, same first and last name as mine and same date of birth, but everything else was changed, and I don't have a middle name."

"Brothers, sisters, mother, cousins?"

"Just me." She swallowed. "As far as I know."

"You waited three months to retrieve important documents from an empty house?"

She'd come to Chicago because she wanted to play music, but on the eve of her audition at the music conservatory, Poppy died alone in their small clapboard house in Peabody. *Music corrupts. Don't ever forget, Sen.* He'd said those words to her just before she left to go north. If she'd listened, Poppy might still be alive. Being in the house where he died made her nauseous.

She looked at Collin and shrugged. "I was busy."

"I understand. Go on."

"The other birth certificate says a man named Thomas Simms is my father and someone named Sonja Albers Simms is my mother. But Loralynn Simms was my mother. She died when I was three but I remember her. I've never heard of Thomas or Sonja. There must be a mix-up. I was born in West Virginia at the County Hospital just outside Peabody. I know it."

"But . . ."

"But this other certificate says I was born in Los Angeles. I've never set foot in California."

"Did you take them to the registry in your county?"

She nodded. "The clerk told me the California one was a fake. He tried to take it away from me, but I raised a fuss until he gave it back."

"What makes you think it isn't a fake?"

"It has an official California state seal on it. I checked. They're both authentic documents."

"What do you think happened?"

"I don't know. I thought maybe I was adopted, but when I researched online, all the adoption sites said the original certificate is sealed by the courts. The names of the adoptive parents are entered on the new certificate, but all the other information is the same. Mine has a different place of birth."

She paused. "Besides everyone in Peabody says I look like Poppy. He had red hair and mine is darker, auburn, I guess. His eyes were blue not green like mine, but I have his freckles and his quick temper." Her face grew hot. "Plus we're both on the short side."

Collin tipped his chair back and folded his hands under his chin. "Doesn't make sense."

"What do you think?"

"One of the certificates is counterfeit, and if I was a gambler, I'd put money on the one issued in Peabody."

"But why the Peabody certificate? Why can't it be the California certificate?" *What if Thomas and Sonja were alive? How would she explain all this to Michael?*

"There is no logical reason to forge a birth certificate naming strangers in L.A. as your parents."

"What is the *logical* reason for faking the Peabody one?"

His voice gentled. "Come on, think about it. The man who claimed you as his daughter would need a birth certificate to prove it. Why would strangers in California risk arrest or a prison sentence to produce a forged document for no purpose? Or at least not one I can see." He dropped his hands and leaned forward. "Are you all right?"

"I knew the California certificate was genuine the minute I pulled it out of Poppy's box of important papers. I just couldn't admit it to myself. My, uh, father is the only family I've ever known. We had our differences, but he loved me as his daughter. I know it." Bewildered, she shook her head. "I don't understand. Why did he do this?"

"I don't know."

Chirp, chirp, chirp. Her cell phone burst into bird song. *Damn!* She'd forgotten about Michael. Her eyes met Collin's.

One corner of his mouth tipped up. Tiny laugh lines curved around his lips. "Do you need to get your phone?"

She slipped her hand into her purse and fished around for her cell. "Excuse me." She retreated into the corridor, shutting the door firmly behind her.

"Hello? Michael?"

"Where are you?"

She stalled for time. "What do you mean?"

"I went by your apartment after work, and you weren't there. You said you'd help me with my speech tonight."

Firing Mr. Atlee was supposed to take five minutes. She planned to be home before Michael arrived. Seneca glanced over her shoulder at the frosted glass. The shadowy head on the other side appeared to be watching her. She ducked out of sight.

"Seneca. Are you there? Is something wrong?"

Poor Michael. He carried the worries of an ailing planet on his shoulders. Some days the weight nearly crushed him. How could she pile on her own minuscule problem and say she loved him? Next spring he was running for the state senate. *No skeletons, Seneca. It's critical. That's how they kill a political movement.*

"I'm fine. I went for a long walk."

"Did something happen at work?"

"Just walking off a bad day. He loaded up my inbox at 4:30. Tomorrow's going to be hell." Administrative assistant to prominent attorney had sounded like an exciting job. Paper shuffler to cheap, egotistical ass proved closer to reality.

"Are you sure?"

"Of course I'm sure." She raised her eyes to the cracked ceiling. Was Poppy watching her fib from his heavenly cloud?

"You've been walking a lot since you got back from Peabody last month."

The scrape of Collin's chair vibrated through the thin wall. "Nothing is going on, Michael. I just forgot." Her temples began to throb. She pressed her hand to her forehead. "I've had a long day."

"Are you almost home?"

Heavy footsteps approached the door. It opened, and Collin's very large, very hunky body filled the doorway. His eyes met hers. He mouthed the word, *Okay?* She held up a finger. *One minute,* she mouthed back. He nodded and turned away. The door stayed open.

She lowered her voice. "It will take me at least an hour to get back to my apartment. I'd understand perfectly if you wanted to bag it and go home."

"I thought this speech was important to us."

Irritation prickled her. "You're being dramatic. It's almost done, and you still have a week before the rally." On the other side of the door, Collin cleared his throat.

"Sorry. I'm just disappointed." A loud sigh blew through the phone. "I'll get something to eat. See you in an hour."

"Can you make it two?"

"An hour. I can't—"

"Two." She turned off the phone.

Seneca ducked back into the office. Collin wore a grave expression, but that darned eyebrow of his lifted again. It was probably how he asked women up to his apartment. "Trouble?"

Her fingers smoothed the folds of her skirt. "Can you take my case?"

"Depends on what you want me to do."

"I want you to find out which certificate is genuine."

"I already told you. It's the California one."

"Where's the evidence? I want to know why. Who are Thomas and Sonja?" She stopped. The eyebrow hadn't moved. "Who am I?"

His eyes softened. "Of course. I'll start right away."

"I need this done yesterday. I've already wasted a month."

"Did you bring the certificates?" He glanced down at her purse.

"They're in my apartment."

He stood. "Let's go."

The sensible part of her brain nudged her. "Mr. Atlee—"

"Collin. If you would prefer to bring them by tomorrow, I understand." He reached over, grabbed a bottle of water from the canvas bag, twisted the cap off and took a long slug. The muscles under his tattoo rippled. They didn't let psychopaths into the Green Berets, did they? Besides, if they didn't get the certificates tonight, she would have to spend eight hours slaving in her airless cubicle before she was free to return with them tomorrow evening. Another day wasted and no closer to finding the truth.

"I guess it would be okay if we hurry. I have an appointment at eight."

In the mood for more Crimson Romance? Check out *Save My Soul* by Elley Arden at *CrimsonRomance.com*.